BLACK BREAD
WHITE BEER

Niven Govinden

The Friday Project
An imprint of HarperCollins*Publishers*
77–85 Fulham Palace Road,
Hammersmith, London W6 8JB
www.harpercollins.co.uk

First published in India in 2012 by Fourth Estate
An imprint of HarperCollins*Publishers* India
a joint venture with
The India Today Group

This paperback edition 2013
I

A catalogue record for this book is
available from the British Library

ISBN: 978-0-00-752986-5

Set in Venetian 301 BT by Sürya
Printed and bound in Great Britain by Clays Ltd, St Ives plc

MIX
Paper from
responsible sources
FSC® C007454

FSC is a non-profit international organisation established to promote
the responsible management of the world's forests. Products carrying the
FSC label are independently certified to assure consumers that they come
from forests that are managed to meet the social, economic and
ecological needs of present and future generations,
and other controlled sources.

Find out more about HarperCollins and the environment at
www.harpercollins.co.uk/green

or *Graffiti My Soul*:

watch ... *Graffiti My Soul* is quite an achieve
en has provided us with a powerful and
ommentary'   *Independent*

and compassionate ... Govinden adopts
argon that immediately communicates the
ntality'   *New*

den effectively creates an atmosphere of
among his characters ... but does it with a t
and real comic flair ... There is much to adm
My Soul'   *Sun*

est but worthwhile novel ... both shocking a
                                              Times Literary

underous rollercoaster of a book, Govinden
violence and depravity of contemporary
usly subversive, happy-slap of a book'

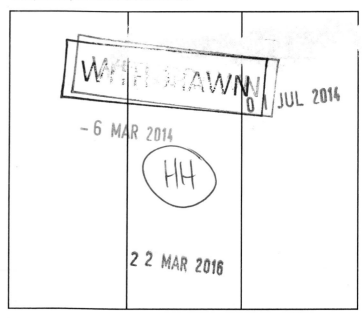

Graffiti My Soul and *We are the New Romantic*

Praise

'One
Govir
social

'Witt
street
old n

'Gov
desp
his e
Graf

'A mo
told'

'In a t
casual
delicic

The two men squat tentatively in their dinghy, floating without enjoyment. There was trouble casting off in the meagre dawn light, one man slipping on shit-splattered cobbles and getting his foot in the water earlier than anticipated. His leg twisting up and out at a sharp angle as he struggled for balance, as if teaching his colleague a new dance move. He is still swearing now, like a teenager, loudly, no restraint; deities and mothers are named in vain. There is no one around to take offence because it is too early for anyone to be out in the park. No one, that is, except a sleepless Amal, sitting on a bench partly hidden by trees.

He watches their nervousness morph into confidence a few metres out, as they paddle with gloved hands towards their destination, the birdhouse in the centre of the lake. Their movements are losing their jerkiness and are becoming smooth and in tandem, a challenge to those Oxford and Cambridge boys who firmly believe that

1

rowing is not a trick that can be learned in five minutes on a glorified duck pond. The man with the dry feet tells a joke that makes the other laugh dirtily. Council-issued fluorescent body-warmers shake with mirth.

But there is still enough grace to put paid to that. The water, algae-ridden but forgiving, absolves their earlier coarseness. Within a couple of minutes they are silent, allowing these unfamiliar sounds to form their new language: the swoosh of the craft, and the drip of their hands, as they plunge in and out. Amal, who cheers-on the boat race most years from a beer tent near Putney Bridge, whose armchair love of sailing extends to an occasional bit-part within the tourist gaggle which breathlessly applauds the arrival of yachts in European marinas, remains silent, unwilling to intrude. The three of them, absorbed with blending the peacefulness of morning to their differing agendas.

At the birdhouse, a bulky, unstable plywood construction turning black with rot, the men throw over a thick sheet of netting. Neither wishes to risk unsteadying the dinghy by getting to their feet, so the throw itself is generated from a position on their knees; one that is weakly weighted and only just lands on its target. Not cut to size, it snags on the pointed roof, and falls over the squat, low doorway. The bottom, knotted in places, frayed in others, trails into the water. There is no checking to see whether there are any visitors inside. There are feathers around the decking, and fast collecting in the net, but this means little to them. They are not Wildlife Protection, but Parks Maintenance, there to do the job asked of them, and no more. They look forward to coffee and bacon rolls in the van and a tick on the list that means they are closer to home.

The netting is of a very dark green, that will appear as black as the birdhouse itself once it weathers, rendering it almost invisible from a distance, from the air. It is also taut, and of a density that a beak would find impenetrable. If there is any concern that a duckling may still be inside, the men do not show it. There is no pause in either paddle movement or direction as they return to bank side, where the van is parked. Only in the final metres does the posture of the dry man shift. His head cranes as far sideways as the balance of the dinghy will allow, the furrow in his brow suggesting a rush job, something overlooked.

Amal, too, listens for a further layer of sound, over the whoosh and plunge – a crackle, a cry, to confirm all that he suspects. Long after the council van has gone, as he shakes his empty cigarette packet and heads for the park gate, he hears it: the tinny, metallic, squall of a youngster, and a rustle of the net. He has the urge to look back, to possibly wade in, and attempt rescue, if rescue is needed, but buries it. Ducks are meat, when it comes down to it. No looking back. He walks away, towards the car, crunching the fag packet in his hand, his teeth repeatedly grazing his lower lip. He is learning that not every life can be saved.

He should clean the car. Have it cleaned. It must be spotless when he goes to collect her. Most of all, it must smell fresh. Already he is planning on leaving some flowers on the back seat to mask both the dry artificial scent of a new car and their own additions over the past day. Seat leather and metal mixed with her perfume was a heady combination that made the drive to work that much more pleasurable. He could sit through two hours of bumper-to-bumper traffic on the M25 with a smile on his face just breathing it in. But this new blend, with the additions of rapid, thick perspiration, and a few drops of urine, and blood, bond too heavily with the intoxicating top notes. With every breath he smells both of them; their fear distilled.

Next to the station is a twenty-four-hour multi-storey car park where two Polish guys offer a valet service from the basement. He has used it a couple of times on commuting days, when he was too late finding a parking space on one of the residential roads. Spotless work, but overpriced. But the car needs it. He feels the urgency of this one task, the stranglehold it seems to have on his guts. He must complete this one productive thing before he meets her.

He is surprised about the looseness of his wallet, how he has been spending so freely since it happened. Thirty pounds on dinner at a gimmicky steakhouse restaurant because he did not want to eat at home alone; twenty pounds at the petrol station off licence; ten pounds at Starbucks which included the purchase of a big band CD which now sits in the glove box, unopened, and finally the twenty-odd he would be charged at the valet place. Claud would tease him in perpetuity if she ever got wind of the spree, emptying out his pockets and looking for moths. Where are they, she would ask. What has happened to my tightwad husband? Is it your birthday? A leap year? She would have, then. Now, who knows?

The Pole is already hard at work waxing an Audi bonnet crisscrossed with blade scratches. Amal is relieved to see that he is the same guy from before, wiry and in his mid-thirties, attentive and eager to please.

'Is no problem. Soon as I finish the Audi.'

As with all men of a certain age there is a brief, flickering appraisal of the state of each other's bodies and hairline.

'Any chance I can cut in? I'll pay more if it'll help.'

'I don't know, sir. I like to finish one car at a time. If I don't use up the wax while it's wet, I have to start the whole thing again.'

'Please. I have to be somewhere . . . and it's important that the car looks nice. Please.'

The last time he detected a pleading note in his tone was yesterday, something he does not like to remember. Both the timbre and the weakness it implies are detestable. It is a slippery slope. He can see that unchecked, how easy it would be lapse into the same sentiment in everyday situations, from cajoling an officious parking attendant, to queue jumping at the post office. Better to dirty himself with money, folding two twenties and pressing them into the waiting palm of the flexible Pole, only to find his bribery is unwanted.

'You have given me too much. Full valet is twenty. Here, go have coffee with the extra money.'

His thanks are conveyed through stutter, another bridge to yesterday, when he struggled to communicate with doctors and the nursing staff. He is also conscious of the Pole finding him a halfwit, and loathes that also. The brain is capable of remembering too much; there are too many links. He wants every action and impulse to differ from his behaviour yesterday. He needs everything to be normal, for both of them.

At the coffee shop he waits, second in line, before ordering double espresso and biscotti, as if he hadn't taken enough comfort in carbs last night. The caffeine jumps starts him, frighteningly fast, making a mockery of his sluggish constitution. Whilst there are no free tables, there are seats dotted around the floor and along the side bar, but he is conscious of sharing the cramped space with strangers, fearful of the need he has to talk. Once he starts he will not be able to stop. No one has been told about Claud, and this is not the place to start.

He takes the biscotti and another espresso back for the Pole.

'OK if I sit in the car? I'm a sad case with nowhere to go.'

There are places, across the road and closer to Richmond Green, but he is known; the price of three married years of melding into the community. The idea of bumping into someone, having to fall into pretence, to sign whatever petition is being championed that week, to care, almost makes him shit in his pants. All he wants to do is hide.

The Pole sees the humour of his situation. Makes a series of rubbing movements with a damp cloth across the windscreen.

'Like you're in the big machine carwash? Sure. I'm finished, anyhow.'

He has been gone twenty minutes and bar the wheels, the car is almost dry. He holds out the paper bag, shakes it towards the Pole with some urgency because he realizes he now longer wants to hold it, wants to be out of there.

'You drink espresso, right?'

'Where I come from, mothers raise children on hot milk. Tea sometimes, but mostly milk. Coffee is more of a luxury. I know people back home, the older people, who still keep jars of Nescafe hidden under their beds! It's still that valuable to them. Our vodka runs like water, but coffee is hidden. Is it the same in your country?'

'My parents come from a tea-growing part of the world. I wasn't allowed to drink anything else.'

'Ha! Thank you, my friend. This is appreciated. You were here before, I think? With the yellow Mini Cooper.'

'My wife's car.'

'Wife, good. Mini is a fine car for a woman, but a man needs something . . .'

His lips broom-broom over the open espresso as he cools it. The noisemaking is as loaded as the coffee, macho-aggressive, but casually so, as basic a part of his constitution as the protons and neurons of his make-up. He imagines how easily this must be deployed in other situations, when chatting up a girl, and later, in bed, something only a man who still finds such posturing difficult to summon would recognize.

'This BMW is a better car. It will impress people when you drive to your important meeting. They will say that this is the car of a successful man. And when they notice how clean it is, they will be even more impressed.'

'I'm not working today. I have to collect my wife from the hospital.'

'She is sick?'

'We had a miscarriage. Yesterday.'

'I am sorry to hear that, brother.'

'Everything's fine, well, she's fine, now. They kept her

in only because there was a spare bed. Monitoring her, you know. Procedure. It's just been a shock.'

'In my country, this is something we do not speak of. It is kept in the preserve of the women.'

'My country too.'

Automatically, he bows to the Indian gene. Though he thinks of himself as educated and enlightened, it is always the pull of the genes that navigates him through crisis, as if there was a state of sense-making that comes solely from the combined force of his parental cells. Before yesterday, he did not think to analyse such superstition. Now, maybe, is the time for its reappraisal.

He is probably a couple of years older than the Pole but should know better. He thinks about telling him that the old ways do not work, that the preserve of women is self-denying crap, but does not wish to destroy the mythology of something he no longer has belief in. He does not have the balls.

His last call to the hospital yesterday was around 11 p.m. After that, he gave himself permission to get stinking drunk. The ward sister lacked her earlier seriousness, lightening his worry. He felt her smiling down the phone on hearing his name, as if she was dying to crack some jokes. He had felt their attention on him, the nurses, checking him out when they wheeled up her to the ward. He was weighed down with empathy.

'Get some sleep, sir. She'll need all the support you've got, tomorrow.' The 'sir', tinged with West Country, and burnished with the weariness of the night shift.

He fell into a brief daydream, wondering at the sheer amount of work to ensure Claud's bed-rest. The silent monitoring that takes place while she sleeps. He was reminded not to call until after eight the next morning because they would be busy with the medicine-giving and breakfast. But now he is anxious at not hearing from them during the night, and figures that half an hour earlier will not hurt.

The ward phone rings out for a good few minutes before the bureaucratic dance begins. A breathless nursing assistant picks up, who then has to summon someone senior because she does not have the recognized accreditations to divulge a patient's condition. The woman does not put him on hold, instead leaving the receiver on the desk while she searches. All the background noises he hears are purely mechanical, rubber wheels on trolleys squelching on rubber-tiled floors, the clang of dropped cutlery, the repeated slamming of lift doors, the wheezy exhalations of a knackered Hoover. There are no human voices at all, as if they are all holding their breath, bound to silence until the receiver is replaced in the cradle.

The staff nurse he eventually speaks to is estuary

accented, and irritated, though she remains factually precise. Claud was given a light sedative just after eleven to help her sleep through the night, she is having breakfast now, managing a sausage and a portion of beans, she will be discharged around ten o'clock once the doctor has made her rounds.

He is aware that he should be camping outside, as all good husbands are expected to do, and maybe he would, if the sheer scale of the building, its aura of benefaction and stoicism, did not cow him. Besides, there are practical domestic affairs he must attend to.

He stinks. Fags, booze, and fried food. No one will understand that he has not been celebrating, that this is his way of coming to terms. He brushes and scrubs like it is his first date. After his shower he passes the broom over the wood floors, and empties the dishwasher. She is unlikely to call the house a tip, will probably not even notice, but if he can do these little things, wipe down the fridge, sweep the path, some good may come.

For all the modernity of their house, a shrine to an architect's vision of what can be done to Edwardian glass and brick, they often cannot wait to be away from it. Whenever they have free time they rush into the arms of the outdoors, they, the unadventurous, as if unwilling to acknowledge it was the wrong house in the first place, that no amount of renovation could make it otherwise.

Past the opening round of house-warming parties, they

have seldom used the place for celebration. Every birthday, weekend, festival, is spent abroad or down at her parents' house in Sussex, a nineteenth-century farmhouse, with its half-acre of mature gardens and a kitchen hearth as wide as a football pitch. It decimates the competition, mocking the faux-authentic picture-book efforts of more suburban homes.

Claud has tried to make their home a warped twin of Liz and Sam's house in the village outside Lewes, turning the reclaimed carriage door into a table, juxtaposing the dominant metallic and stone of the kitchen; the argyle knitted rugs thrown over wooden floors; and deco mirror sets in the bedroom, above each nightstand, and across her dressing table, as if, like her mother, she is unconsciously playing the part of a silent movie star, the aspiring city girl trapped by marriage in the country, with only her glamorous trinkets to remind of more sophisticated times.

That is not to say the house has no warmth. All the homes that line the street have a similar square-fronted handsomeness, and theirs is no different. It is cluttered and lived-in. Radio, television, and the iPod docks do their part in filling space. There is nothing forbidding about the 50's-style welcome mat on the front step, all sunrise and exclamation point, nor the silver-framed Om hanging above the door in the hall, exuding Eastern peace and radiance. Indeed, he has hurried home most nights, yearning for the sofa and the feeling of Claud cuddling into the nook of his arm and shoulder. But something is missing; they both know it. The arrival of an intangible object or presence that will make sense of their choices and hard work.

The pile of magazines cries out for the recycling box. He takes them out, having a final smoke as he does so, lifting one from the packet stashed amongst the upturned ceramic pots that litter the patio's far reaches. It is the unwritten rule of twenty-first-century gift-giving, that a guest should never arrive without a token for the garden. They have more pots than they know what to do with, filled with plants that need little maintenance, woody herbs and tall reedy bamboos, and neatly patterned around the plot, like a super-sized, organic solitaire. The unwanted remainder should be dumped in the garage by rights, a job that continues to escape his mind, until the point when he's hiding and retrieving fags. Claud often jokes that they should recycle them as gifts, if only they knew which person had given which pot.

Ordinarily, when hopes are not being lost he smokes one, two cigarettes a day. It helps. He likes to think that he's unashamed of needing a crutch, but still goes to pains to conceal it, not wanting her to think that he hasn't agreed whole-heartedly with her plans: organic food, chemical-free detergents, regular, moderate exercise. Conception is something to be taken seriously, needing as much preparation as a marathon.

'We're in our thirties, Amal. I've messed-up my periods with over-dieting. Your metabolism is slowing to a stop with all that pizza. We're not single people any more. We have to get a grip of ourselves, make changes.'

He has read the many printouts she leaves on the kitchen counter, that say an abundance of fish, and Brazil nuts are good for his sperm. Many cloves of raw garlic, too. His breath is pungent enough to wither vine fruits, forcing a dependency on extra-strong mints in the office. Other than red wine, alcohol, particularly beer, is banned. So is masturbation. Bread is gluten free, dairy limited. A glass of water must be drunk every hour; supplements are taken twice a day: a multi-vitamin, iron, selenium, omega 3, and aspirin. His piss is sent off for analysis, his stools discussed most mornings whilst he cleans his teeth, something he never thought he would be doing with a white woman. They spend four weeks on this treadmill before she lets him near her, the time it takes to convince that they have eliminated the worst of their collective toxins. Penance for their self-absorbed, shag-around twenties. He leaves her printouts too, which go unread: studies which show how excessive ejaculation can lead to prostate cancer.

'We can worry about your prostate later. We can leave it to our kids to take care of us.'

All that matters is the here and now: the diet, sticking to the plan. She wants to make a baby with the best cellular development, with the cleanest, tox-free constituent elements. She does not want to leave anything to chance.

Now, while he waits for ten o'clock, he is intent on toxing-up, filling his boots with carcinogens. Fag in mouth as he finally shifts the pots into the garage like she has been asking for weeks, months. Do your bit, boy. Move your arse. The clean way has not worked, so maybe this will be better. Even before she returns, he feels the disappointment, self-blame, hanging in the air, but it does not seem irreparable. It is nothing that faith cannot fix.

 ⚜

He is parking up at the hospital when Hari calls him. It is close to ten and there has been no word from the hospital. He figures he should muscle in on the ward so he can be present when the doctor arrives. He has pulled himself together. Looks respectable. His shoulder is steady, ready to take her weight.

'You'll have to be quick, mate. I'm about to go into a meeting.'

The work brush-off is a default setting they are attuned to, nothing that can be picked up on. His tone is curt, and vaguely irritated. They all behave like this between nine and six.

'Oh. I thought you'd be at the hospital.'

'Why would I be at the hospital?'

'Because of Claud. You called me last night, remember?'

It feels as if someone has drawn a curtain, making the hint of a secondary unease — headache to a bellyache — tangible. He remembers the close noise of the steakhouse restaurant, a birthday party on the table next to him, of having to move towards the revolving doors and still shouting to be heard. He remembers gabbling about how scared he was. Crying. What he cannot recall is Hari's voice, or pulling up his number. He could have been talking to anyone.

'I probably shouldn't even be calling, but I just wanted to see if you guys were ok. If there's anything I can do.'

Men do not have best friends the way women do. It is too co-dependent a state, one that can overwhelm the basic masculine need for secrets and freedoms. But if pushed, he would admit that Hari falls somewhere in that area, solid and omnipotent. Hari brought him and Claud together in the first place. Match-made his new work colleague with his university buddy, something that seems to have given him a vested interest in their marriage. Makes him wonder now, about the crying, whether it was actually Hari's he remembers, and not his?

He showered Hari with thanks in those early days. Thanks for working with this amazing woman he couldn't keep his hands off. You're a mate. Thanks for weaning him off those shady nightclub girls he fruitlessly chased for most of his twenties. He gave thanks for every time she laughed at him and his badly constructed jokes which still remain all incidentals and no punch-line. When she applauded his cooking, and for not assuming he made curry every night of the week.

He thanked her for the pawing and growling that came after dinner, and often before. For the little sounds she made. The little sounds he made. For being obsessed with her red hair, especially the way it looked when it caught the lamplight in the bedroom, deep, concentrated, as if her head had already been cast in bronze, timeless and luminescent. For not wanting to be away from her, for needing to catch every word she said, whether flighty stream of consciousness or good, plain sense. He thanked him for hooking him up with a girl who was cleverer, who was on a faster career path and earned more. Who spoke with experience when she said that it was better to sit things out with his firm than look to be the big fish in smaller ponds. Who did not shy away from talking about money, but equally did not allow it to become the elephant in the room. Thanked him for the energy, the whirlwind. Days speeding past towards languid, dreamy weekends, a perfect mix of domesticity and fantasy. Thanked him for her silliness, that she was a goofball for all her careerist seriousness. That she was always up for a spontaneous water fight, and karaoke, but drew the line at descending into sickly baby voices with him. But most of all, he thanked Hari for putting her in his universe, wondering how he could have previously existed without her. He was soppy with love, then.

When he was finishing his master's during his early twenties, he was smacked around the head by a group of kids at the bus stop, suffering a broken nose and fractured eye socket. The kids hauled a mere twelve pounds and a prehistoric mobile phone, which he was about to get rid of anyway. He thinks about the phone call he made to Hari from the hospital, his voice as cracked as his face, and the discomfort this brewed in him. He does not want to be viewed with compassionate eyes for a second time, nor any further prying into the state of their marriage. They do not need help. They are fine.

Privacy is needed. Ignorance. Hari's compassion is simply the first wave, the ripple along the surf. They will be drowned many times over before others have finished expressing their sympathy.

'Does anyone else know?'

'I haven't had time to think. Not even our parents know yet.'

'I can ring around if it'll make things easier.'

'No. This is Claud's shout. Something we need to keep to ourselves for the time being.'

He has a feeling when the signal fails, fortuitously, the phone masts banished from the hospital's immediate radius, that he will be avoiding Hari for a very long time, now seeing the point of distance between friends.

This is not the plan. She has already been discharged. He sees her, unexpectedly, as he walks up the ramp towards the entrance and works hard to keep his face from crumbling. She is sitting on a bench, reading a leaflet, her overnight bag wedged between her feet. Even from this distance he sees what change the night has brought, how she seems to have shrunk by degrees, her wraparound coat, a recent prized buy, now appearing several sizes too big for her. No longer following the contours of her body, its bagginess gives her a wizened quality, the double knot tied at the waist making her appear swaddled. Bleached out by sunlight, she is so pale as if to emphasize her blood loss, though the bed curls and the detailed embroidery across the coat breast give her a gothic quality; a vampire in urgent need of food. Her eyelids are red with lack of sleep, in spite of the staff nurse's earlier report. Sockets are marginally sunken and bags more pronounced. As she lifts her hand to turn the pamphlet, he notices a series of angry blotches floating across her hand, suggesting that every part of her body is suffering the loss. Only the glow of her hair remains defiant, refusing to mourn.

'I thought the doctor wasn't seeing you until later. They told me not to get here until ten.'

'They've a busy day in theatre. Wanted to get me out of the way.'

'What did she say?'

'Same as yesterday. Please can you take me home, now?'

She will not be kissed; rises and walks down the ramp before he has a chance to tell her where the car is. The leaflet, ditched on the bench, is for counselling. He too chooses to leave it.

The drive is difficult. She does not want to talk. Does not want the radio. They had talked on the drive up yesterday. Reassuring talk that willingly ignored the sudden blood loss in the bathroom. Useless, ignorant talk that pooh-poohed the writings of medical practitioners, and played for her trust. Now there is no right to speak unless spoken to. He feels her tightening up against him, watches the tautness of her mouth as she keeps it all in. It is as if the easiness they once shared, the ability to be comfortable with one another has been lost with the baby.

The bunch of sunflowers he believed to be casual and not loaded with meaning are registered briefly, then ignored. Nor does the grey angora blanket thrown over the passenger seat please her.

'Worried about messing the car? Why doesn't that surprise me?'

Her laugh is grim and pained.

'I thought you might be cold.'

'I've got this coat. Don't need wrapping up in cotton wool.'

Why are you holding it then, he wants to ask, stung. He is expecting her to bite but is still unprepared for it when the sharp words come, so busy was he in his head to make everything right. He must not let her behaviour cloud his judgement or feeling. What has happened has been harder on her than he could ever imagine. The doctor said as much last night. Anger, guilt, and blame must be compassionately received. Only then will she open up.

He can do it if he tries. See past the scorn manifest on her face, and the strangulation in her voice each time she addresses him; even if its tension is like a single wire held firm at the base of his neck, ready to slit his throat at the first thoughtless remark. For the first time in their marriage he is frightened and aware that he does not know her. But he can forget that, fear crushed under Pirelli tyres, when her breath loses its shallowness and becomes deeper, bringing some warmth into the frozen cabin; when she touches his shoulder lightly and says, 'Can we take a drive though Richmond Park? I'm not ready to go home yet.'

'Sure. What do you want, hills or deer?'

'Deer, I think.'

'Why not? We can take the route we took the other week. That way we get some hills too. Best of both worlds.'

They drive though Richmond Gate, whose imposing presence, tall and unencumbered by trees or outbuildings, always seems to dwarf and belittle all who enter, then left, towards sparser areas of the park, Ham, Sheen, and Pen Ponds, away from walkers and anywhere where there may be groups of mothers and small children. He has driven in a roundabout way from the hospital, taking a series of back roads to avoid two primary schools for this very reason.

He sees her looking for where the deer converge. Her eyes intently study thick growths of bracken and fern, craning her neck across both sides of the road as she peers through dark, mature copses for any sign of movement. He wonders whether it is the creatures themselves she wants to see, or just a confirmation of their camouflage, that maybe she too wishes to hide.

But there are no deer to be seen on their tour, only a panorama of discarded water bottles and a trail of tanned cyclists, Australian or South African, streaming through the foliage. He watches as her eyes lock onto the cyclists' wheels weaving along the dust track, taking in the lightness of those machines, and the speed and the agility of those powering them. The BMW is an unwieldy beast by comparison, a useless lump of metal, leather and angora, pitifully unable to fly her away.

'Pretty, isn't it?' he says, uselessly, unable to bring himself to mention the cyclists, spectacularly male and thundering with sun-nurtured virility.

'Not without the wildlife. It looks like a giant garden otherwise.'

'I thought rabbits were meant to be lucky, not deer,' he says, and immediately realizes it is the wrong thing to say, that luck should not be brought into anything, should never be mentioned again.

'I tell you what, Claud. I'll get some venison in for dinner if we don't see any. Knock-up one of my specials. How does that sound?'

The hand on the shoulder again. A softening.

'Amal, you don't have to do anything special because you think it'll cheer me up. I'm fine.'

'Really? You're fine.'

'Yes. I am. I will be. Stop worrying.'

On the second stage of their honeymoon, a weekend at a country house on the edge of Dartmoor, a late-Victorian decompression chamber following three weeks in Mexico, their suite had been studded with several stag heads won from various county hunts. Claud had tried to hang from one of them whilst he was eating out of her. There was no chandelier in the room so this was the next best thing. They were adventurous, then. Sun-spoilt and happy, he remembers her laughing with fear that she would fall, with a ten-weight of antlers bearing down upon her, before giving in to a deeper, more localized pleasure. Now he could not get her to eat venison. They were in trouble.

'We can't have supper at home, anyway. I told Mum and Dad we'd go round.'

'When was this?'

'Few minutes ago, whilst I was waiting for you. You know how they like to call first thing on Friday before they do the weekend shop. I said we were treating ourselves to a day off, which is why she caught me on the mobile.'

'You didn't tell them?'

'Their washing machine's packed up and Dad needs help fitting the new one. Too tight to pay for delivery and installation. It's been sitting in the boot of his car since Tuesday, Mum said. They were waiting until the weekend to ring us.'

'I'll pay for someone. You need to rest, Claud, not go racing down to Sussex. One day's rest, at least. Please.'

'Sleeping isn't going to make anything come back, Amal. It's an afternoon and possibly some supper, that's all. I've been resting since we found out I was pregnant. I'm sick of lying down.'

'What are you going to tell them?'

'Nothing. As far as they're concerned, I'm still pregnant.'

'Look, I . . .'

'This isn't up for discussion. I'm not ready, all right?'

He feels the cheese-cutting wire again, sliding back and forth across his throat, making it impossible to argue. Understanding the secrets of marriage is knowing when to pick your battles. This is not the time to be charging forth, discussing the merits of getting everything out in the open. She will not tolerate any of that. Though still weak from the blood loss, she remains capable of eating him alive. He is simply there as muscle, nothing more.

'Stop the car! There! See him?'

For the lightness it momentarily brings to her face, he is prepared to see anything. Nestled within a copse at the foot of the hill leading to Ham Gate, he sees a wall of browning ferns and their manipulation by the wind, nothing more. If, as she says, there is indeed a pair of brown eyes hidden within, he is either too short-sighted, or too thick-headed to find them. His silence is taken for zoological studiousness, something he does little to correct. If this is what makes her happy, let her be happy. They sit there together, seeing differently, finally comfortable.

She is hungry. They share a bacon roll and a choc ice from the van trading in the car park. The salt from the bacon and the sweet from the ketchup fill every pocket of the car, imbibing a sense of homeliness and safety which shows up the poor work of the wilting sunflowers.

'If something like this doesn't give you the excuse to eat junk food, I don't know what does,' she says, mid-mouthful. A drop of ketchup wobbles on her cheek. Ordinarily he would lick it off.

Claud has not touched pork for over two years. Not even long weekends in Grenada or Barcelona, touring time-worn Jamon bars could persuade her to accompany her glass of Olorosso with a slice of Serrano, Iberico, or Chorizo. She worried about the effect of too much red meat on their future offspring even then.

'Mmm. This is great, love. Good thinking.'

Amal does not confess to his lapse at last night's trashy restaurant, not wishing to break the fragile equilibrium. He paid with cash so she never need know. She devours her half of the roll in a flash, and then eats the bulk of his, making him buy another so that they can further indulge in the goodness of hot food. Pre-empting her, he comes back with doubles, piled with onions and extra condiments.

He needs to keep feeding her, he realizes. Fill her up with food. Stuff her guts until she has to sleep sitting up, too shot with cholesterol and bad sugars to think about the other cavernous spaces in her body. Claud is a fine cook, has looked after him well, but he is just as good when he gets on the stove. The range is the only gadget that really interests him, other than his iPhone. It is back to the Indian gene, the one that believes the kitchen is the heart. He will cook until food is coming out of her gullet, absorbing everything, including the need to feel.

The choc ices have been dredged from the bottom of the freezer where they have frozen solid, but after the greasy bacon they are still needed and devoured. Their taste is grainy and synthetic, recalling something conceived in laboratories rather than the cute provincial dairy pictured on the wrapper. If this is the kind of crap they feed kids, then theirs has had a lucky escape. God! If he had said that aloud, there would have been a repeat of last night, a series of choked sobs in the car after the restaurant. Him making a fool of himself in front of her; just what he has been trying to avoid. Jesus, it is hard. His foot is on the gas before he has finished his final mouthful. A bounce of the chassis as the wheels lightly skid over the gravel. It is better to drive than remember.

The house welcomes them. Mid-morning sunlight pours from windows and seeps through brick, making what was previously cold appear golden and pleasantly holiday-burnt. Maybe they are carne-drunk with the bacon and visions of feral deer, but it suddenly feels like a place worth staying in; their previous criticisms fading with every degree on the sundial. They are both pleased to be there.

The sun-blush makes her admit the obvious, that she is exhausted, and he is left to potter in the kitchen whilst she has an hour's nap upstairs. He busies himself on the tasks he thoughtlessly missed earlier: hosing out the dustbin and cleaning the oven, though he questions how else he can distract himself once the house is completely clean.

England is playing India in the second Test. The commentary from the radio on the kitchen counter is low, making every exclamation and cry of disbelief sound half-hearted and whispered. He resists the lulling effect of hearing bat against ball, the slide of shoe across the crease, and the hoot and stagger of short, concentrated runs. England are having a good day, driving mercilessly at the Indian advantage. The team is working methodically, tirelessly, attempting with every duck and strike to erase the fortune and legacy of their hosts. They need to keep up this batting pace and level of attack for the rest of the day if they are to cause any great upset. The determination that is reported to him via the leathery-throated commentator and his mangled euphemisms suggests that this will be the case.

He thinks about Sam listening to the match down in Sussex, from the car probably, as he jealously guards his cheapest-of-the-range washing machine, and wonders whether he too will be drawing the same conclusions. In spite of his ignorance about what has happened to the baby, will he enjoy the sportsmanship of the first Test, or will he only think of what is happening on an Indian field as a reflection of his feelings towards Amal, a desire to drive him out?

She comes downstairs after half an hour, her face clouded with a familiar anxiety that sets his mind racing to yesterday.

'We need to change the upstairs toilet. I can't use that bathroom until we do.'

'I can do that.'

'I mean it. I can't go there. Our baby died there.'

'It's ok. I'll sort it. Soon as we get back from Lewes. Use the downstairs in the meantime.'

Like a child he trundles her in the direction of the second bathroom, inexplicably situated off the downstairs hall. When they bought the house they laughed at the planner's logic of it, a whirlpool bath and bog just across from the living room when there was ample and more discreet square footage towards the back of the house.

But they agreed about its practicality in anticipation of visiting in-laws and other guests. Situated almost centrally and therefore catching both morning and evening light, it would have made a fine office, or even a boys room, where they could have placed a dark leather sofa, a shamefully tacky beer fridge, and installed one of those pull-down screens to play games or watch DVDs. Now he is thankful that they did not.

He has a case of delayed reaction, flinching every time she talks about the baby. His moves are discreet, whilst she is behind the toilet door, or as now, once she is tucked-up in bed with a kiss on the forehead. This is the first time she has allowed his lips to touch her. Even in the hospital at her most fearful, she was only comfortable with the firm grip of his hand crushing hers, as if the connection between them was no more tenuous than neighbour, work colleague, or passer-by. But safely away from her he flinches, unguarded, like the holder of a nervous tic. The certainty of her words seems to visibly play before him as he waits for the plumber's website to open on his laptop. He tries hard to concentrate, thinking that whatever he orders now can be delivered, installed even, by the time he gets back, so long as he leaves the keys next door and is able to persuade Claud that a night spent over in Lewes is the best medicine. But everything is overshadowed by b-a-b-y.

Unlike her he has no clarifying definition for what they

have lost. Something which is not yet a baby but more than a cluster of cells, a mere six weeks of growth, and is responsible for an unseen, immeasurable emptiness. They themselves have only known for sure these past three weeks, so how can so much hope grow in that time? How does the work of twenty-one days so effectively decimate all the hurdles that stand before their vulnerability?

A complete miscarriage, the doctor called it, pleased with its neatness and lack of invasive surgery required. A complete miscarriage, more common than realized in the early stages of the first trimester: as if that explained everything, closed the lid on their bewilderment. But concrete fact, the overbearing weight of statistics, is a poor cover for soft tissue. It holds no weight against the physical ache he sees in Claud as well as the tightness he tries to ignore in his own chest. How does ten centimetres of cell and pliable bone get to do that?

Though it is not yet midday he has a good swig from one of the bottles in the cupboard, white rum or a flavoured vodka, cloudy but citrusy sharp, before forcing himself to swallow the remainder of the salmon and fennel salad in the fridge. Crisp, peppery, and heavy with garlic, it obliterates all evidence of his alcohol-driven weakness.

He has never been a big drinker. It is one of the things Claud liked about him from the start.

'I only want to get serious with a guy who isn't going to

blow his salary on buying rounds for the boys, under the pretext of entertaining clients. I've been with twits like that before.'

This is another thing to mull over at a later date, how easy it is to take comfort in drink. Tomorrow he can repent, today he needs haziness for the drive, a slight, numbing touch to ease the pressure of two hours on a cramped A-road. She needs him to protect her. He needs vodka to make that a possibility, if only he had the bottle to be that kind of man.

Claud is persuaded to take half a sleeping pill so she can sleep most of the way. The siesta time in the house has been a failure. There was no way she was going to relax once she got upset about the toilet. He hears her talking over the cricket, where the wiliness of the subcontinent's bowling technique crushes the now pedestrian bulldog effort, in a swift display of shock and awe. In spite of the pleasure this gives him, thinking of the blow it must deliver to Sam's spirit, he still wants England to win. Fuck the cricket test theories, England is his team, is all.

He hears her on the phone before they leave the house. Her voice is low but has lost the dead tone of before. Whoever is on the other end has dragged lightness out of her, something he has had over twenty-four hours to perfect and was unable to accomplish. When he walked down the church aisle three years ago, a newly baptized Christian – a page note to the cricket test, a secondary gesture to please Liz and Sam – he married not just her, but her girlfriends as well; those ready to jump in and complete all the things that he cannot do.

This is his turn to feel the b-a-b-y, a collection of cells ripped from him, no longer their precious secret, but a story to be gossiped about over sweetish cocktails and wine coolers. There was a bitter yet muddled sense of disloyalty after sharing it with Hari, but there is something more agonizing about the permanence of girl talk. With every detail spilled down the phone he feels their child slipping from an imaginary grasp, and disappearing like a dream.

'I told Jen. She texted me and it all came out.'

'It's good that you're talking about it,' he says, angry with himself that he is unable to stop feeling betrayed. 'Jen's a good person to have around.'

'I couldn't stop talking once I started. Sorry.'

'Nothing to apologize about. It helps to share it.'

'You should talk to someone too. Ring Hari.'

So talking is advocated, championed, in fact, so long as they do not do it with each other. They sit side by side at the breakfast counter unable to look each other in the eye.

'I don't need to speak to anyone. I'm fine.'

Her passive aggression weighs heavily on his shoulders,

creeping across his front in a choke-hold. He resists. All too often has she used the same tactic.

I've told Clare about the engagement. Do you want to tell someone? Hari? Mum wangled it out of me that we're trying for a baby. You might as well tell your parents now so that we're in sync. Or maybe Hari if you don't want to tell them straight away. But you should tell someone.

It is the most comfortable, easy-reaching tool in her box of tricks, so he understands why she still clings on to it, the way the collection of cells should have stayed attached to her insides.

Her reliance on these things is admirable, how she expects him to call Hari right away, while she is still there, so that every nuance of the conversation can be analysed, then corrected. She was the same last week when he called the service people to get the digital TV box looked at. Bossiness has propelled her through higher education and a fast-track in her career. It gets results. Why should she be any different now? But it should be. Some things should be different between them. He sees how such a move can bang nails into a coffin further down the marriage. His parents. Liz and Sam.

She is crying again as he packs the car. He knows her tears come more from a frustrated place, because he ignored her attempts to call Hari, than anything to do with the lost collection of cells. Office cynicism does not stay in the office. It is a part of every aspect of their home. The muffled package of sniff and sob resonates as loudly as any wailing for the way it follows him outside, but he carries on with packing the car. He speaks quietly to the neighbour about the plumber, and goes about his business; not going to her, knowing she is still not ready to be touched.

Again there is nothing to listen to. She should not be woken on the journey, aside from a gentle tap on the shoulder when they wind up the drive in Lewes. Their story has been concocted. There is no reason to discuss it endlessly. They are making the most of a well-earned long weekend. She is pregnant. They are happy.

Driving through the country will hurt with its constant reminders of plant in bud. Everything has the ability to reproduce but them. He prefers it on the motorway where concrete has killed all life. Black and grey, miles of it, make everything better. It is time to reaffirm his faith in hard, physical objects: the road, his Blackberry and iPhone. There is nothing to be had in believing in organics.

Six-lane traffic, its smoothness and gentle contours has a blank, hypnotic quality. Something about the road erases, forgives. He sees now why men drive and the attraction of long distances. How two hours on a clear road is probably more therapeutic than a year's worth of visits to any shrink.

The hospital offers counselling the way doctors hand out pills, automatically, by the handful. How much time did women in the past spend with a psychologist between their pregnancies and miscarriages? Were they given the luxury of a week-off from housework and radio silence from relatives in order to recuperate? People got on with things, then. Everything about their own upset, the clawing in his gut, her muffles, is by comparison lazy, self-indulgent, and most likely, deserved.

But maybe it is in the nature of women to dust themselves down and carry on. He can see her back in the office next week, glued to the Blackberry, allowing herself no time to reflect. Maybe it is only the men who have let the modern age weaken their resilience, crying into baked goods and wallowing into beer. But everything about her knotted sleep in the car makes that a lie. She feels it all.

Trouble comes when he stops for a toilet break at a Road Chef a couple of miles before the A21. She wakes and follows him, half-running across the car park to catch up, which generates a pang of fear that something might be wrong with her insides.

'I need to change the dressing. Nothing for you to worry about.'

It is the first he has heard about dressings. All this time he has avoided looking at her abdomen, as he fears this will wound her, though he badly wants to; to study the contours of her body, and look for evidence of smoothness where a bump was once imagined and fussed over. But she is on to him, reads the unsophisticated voyeurism knotted across his brow, and keeps her hands folded over her tummy as she walks. Fingers locked, elbows straight, her moves are geisha, doll-like. She wears a t-shirt and the patterned mohair cardigan he bought her for Christmas. Mohair on mohair. The whole car park knows about it. When she made to get out of the passenger seat, the static squeal bounced from one vehicle to the next.

Ignoring the tightness in his bladder, he stands at the entrance to the Ladies, as he is trained to do. He sees aqua tiles from floor to ceiling and detects the same family of smells as those from the hospital. He does not know what he is waiting for. All the damage has already been done. Besides, he is exhausted with having to be the man of the relationship. He is unsure how much reserve he has left if he is called upon for the second time.

There is a reason Claud discharged herself before he arrived. She wanted to keep all the medical details between herself and the doctor. The dressing is only one secret they share. He suspects others.

'Wives keep secrets from their husbands,' said his best man on his wedding day. Hari is the expert, shagging one frustrated wife after another; a Lone Ranger, regularly pulling up in his Land Rover at the cafés most of them use after the school run.

Amal is unsure that secrecy can exist in a marriage as

close as theirs. When he has every breath pattern and face pore memorized, predicting how she will toss and turn in her sleep – right then left, curl and back; in the midst of urgent, concentrated sex, in sync, when the concept of possession is anathema, to the point where he feels that he actually becomes her; and when, as he cooks, he knows how each particular food will taste for her, where are the secrets? Where in their airy, uncluttered house can they be held?

He was stupid to think that cleaning was the priority, obsessed as he was with staying busy with his hands. He should have camped outside the hospital, greeting the doctor with chair sweat and a furry tongue. He should have left no opportunities for secrets, not because he is possessive, but because he knows that secrets will hurt them. They have had to make the conscious effort to be transparent with one another. It is one of the essential requirements of a marriage such as theirs, to avoid misunderstandings and the breeding of corrosive resentment. It means therefore that any gripes are put down to superficial, bachelor selfishness, laziness, or lapses in judgement; trifles that can be rowed over and then quickly resolved.

His plan is to wheel her back to the car as soon as she reappears, avoiding the MacDonalds concession, KFC, and the children's play area. The precautions, should he have to explain them, are ridiculous. There is no emotional meltdown waiting to happen in the space between the mechanical fire engine and giant revolving tea cup. She is too empty to do that. He only wants to hide these things from her for as long as he can. Pretend that there are no children in the world, that they are as rare as baby eagles or panda cubs. Make it seem like it is a miracle for everybody.

But something about the new dressing energizes her. She is not to be shaken off, wanting to visit the shop to pick up a token for Pat. The gift store, opposite all that he wishes to disappear, is as claustrophobic and depressing as any he has encountered on the side of the motorway. Still, there is a shine to Claud that the flat strip-lighting cannot diminish; perked up by the piles of outdated CDs and tartan car blankets.

'Two for £25 it says. I could use one in the car now and give the other to Mum.'

'It's terribly made. Look at the label. Says it's a wool-poly blend. Listen to how it crinkles up. It's like plastic.'

'I like them. They're pretty.'

'Since when have you been into tartan?'

'It's not a question of being into. Tartan's something everyone's brought up with in Britain.'

Those final two words, randomly chosen to put him in his place. His parents were not born in England. He wouldn't understand. It is something from Sam's repertoire, picked up so thoughtlessly, used so often. She does not know that she is even doing it; does not know what it means.

'It might not seem like a big deal, but we cannot do Sunday lunch without Yorkshires. Bring that dinner out from an English pub kitchen and they'd have your balls on a plate . . . Yes, I know it sounds like the cast of Billy Smart's circus, but my daughter really does need four ushers, two page boys, and two flower girls. That's how it's done in this part of the world.'

Bigots do not raise ugliness in their daughters, just a certainty of where their place is, and what is right. For all her education, wit, compassion, Claud is guaranteed to fall into the tartan setting every once in a while, usually when they are snappy and close to argument. It is as natural as temper, right as rain.

He thinks of some of Puppa's friends from the '70s, and their marriages. A stream of white wives crying in Ma's kitchen surprised at being beaten for similar displays of indigenous expression. There are one or two husbands he remembers in particular, chubby Indian beefcakes, stinking of the card table and taking no shit. Filthy tempers. The kind of men who would think nothing of giving the woman a slap beside the lopsided pile of wool-poly tartan blankets.

Slapping is not an option, inconceivable, but there are other forms of cruelty. He can protect her until she is smothered by concern, for example. Or, more easily, he can throw her to the wolves, leaving her to fend for herself once he remembers that he still needs a slash. A party of school kids are stampeding towards the crisp aisle. Thirty of them, fresh from the cramped hire coach and ready to use their feet.

'See you at the car. Probably easier.'

He watches as she takes a deep breath, kidding himself that it is the choices between blanket colours which is making her cheeks flush and her arm imperceptibly wobble. Red-green, red-yellow, blue-green, blue-yellow, red-black. He waits only until the first of the children stream around her in their quest for confectionary, seeing how she almost has to force her head to stay directed on the job in hand.

The options are St. Leonards or villages. She chooses villages, knowing where the roads will lead: the cottage outside Robertsbridge where they spent their first weekend together, the antique market at Rye where they chose her engagement ring, the church overlooking Lewes Common where they married. All the significant points in their relationship have taken place in her part of the country. There was never any validity to spending time in Leicestershire.

Up there, in the Midlands, they are all aware of what is

happening, how sons are lost after marriage, cruelly appropriated into the wife's family; the opposite of what occurred to their subcontinental forebears. It is the price paid for marrying English girls, in spite of their vehement protestations to the contrary. But it is a phenomenon not simply restricted to skin tone. Amal's other friends, white-skinned and robbed of voice, are also in the same boat: pussy-whipped. Life is good so long as the missus is happy.

He has lost count of the key events that he has missed: the wedding of a second cousin which clashed with the opportunity for a free long-weekend in Milan, the puja at his auntie's new house to banish spirits being cancelled out because Liz and Sam needed help looking for a new car. It is a long list of incompletes.

It is not that Claud lacks interest in his family – the euphemism for culture, because to call it culture would be to admit there are more than cute gaps between the sexes causing difficulties in their marriage – she keeps a better calendar of events than he does. She reads books about Empire, Partition and fundamentalism, drags him to every shitty Bollywood film that plays at the multi-screen, and calls his mother independently at least once a week. The problem lies in their absence, them not being available the way other people's children are; those who made the decision to stay in around Leicester. Ma and Puppa feel robbed of the opportunity to arrive at their son's house unannounced, to use spare keys to fiddle and poke around whilst they are at work, and to summarily summon one or the other during the onset of perceived indigestions and illnesses.

There is no cooking daal and roti and leaving them in Tupperware boxes in the fridge, no unofficial, covert fertility blessings they can perform using only a bell and a stick of incense, then hurriedly airing the house before their departure. All they know is that their son and his wife are never around, becoming harder to reach, and that after three years of marriage there is still no grandchild.

Neither subject can be brought up, and they have to rely on jibes from other distant relatives to do the job they do not have the stomach for. They feel too far away from their son to rock the boat. They are at the age where they only want to end phone conversations on a happy note, unsure of what the night will bring. And so they keep their tone as light as they can without breaking into hysteria, leaving Amal to read the neuroses behind every piece of weather observation and gossip.

'It's been cold, hasn't it,' typically conveys everything.

He knows they were never disappointed in him marrying Claud. A man must pick the woman he wants. There is no alternative in this decade. Raise your children. Let them go. Choose your moments.

Liz and Sam have seen them twice since they announced the news. His parents have not had the privilege of blessing the stomach, instead made to toast over the speakerphone due to a clashing working weekend, followed by their annual trip to Kolkata. The foremost guilt he feels is that they have been denied the sight of her, of the two of them, glowing with iron-rich supplements, and uncensored optimism. Some of the squealing down the phone expressed that, but not their hope. He still feels ashamed that he did not do enough to accommodate their seeing it. Taken a bloody day off. Gone out of his way. But there was plenty of time, went the rationale, close to a year of congratulations and microscopic study to come from the immediate family.

'Let's stretch it out a bit, the victory lap,' Claud suggested at the time, not worried about holding back until amnio results and first scans, just wary of the weight of attention, and the likely threat of intrusion. She saw a similar display of the diplomatic back and forth that preceded their wedding, the collection of cells, its rooting inside her, acting as a reminder that family obligations were inescapable. His family, inexorable.

Relaying the news by phone or skype to Kolkata, where aunts, uncles, and layabout cousins would most likely crowd around, effectively erasing all notions of privacy, did not faze him, for there was some comfort knowing that Ma and Puppa now expected his every emotional extreme to be delivered via phone lines. Whatever was not revealed would be passed on at a later date by Hari, a compulsive, unrepentant gossip.

There was freedom in allowing them to hear the faintest marital spat as the state-of-the-art broadband line hissed and crackled, like bone-dry kindling being used to fire up a plus-size cauldron.

'We are happy with whatever you want to do, so long as you make this baby a child of God, any God,' they said, a week ago, fourteen days after the news had been broken. Broken, like it was a product launch, or international event.

'Health and happiness are already accounted for. There is no excuse for a deficiency of either in this day and age. But spiritual plans must be consciously put into place. The child will lack a dimension in life if it lives without a God, any God.'

'Like Aishwarya Rai? I hear they worship her in some parts of London.'

'Don't make a joke of this, Amal. We're being serious.'

'I know, Ma. This is something we'll look into. There's plenty of time.'

'Look into? This is not the scouts or girl guides, Amal. These things have to be decided from the outset.'

'Ma, Puppa, we will definitely not run away from this. Leave it to me to handle Amal.'

They argued about it later, long after parental fears were eased in Kolkata and the speakerphone, shredded with effort, finally cut out. It was the only time during the twenty-one days that they raised their voices with one another over conflicting plans for the collection of cells.

'Our baby should have dual teaching, not just made into a Hindu,' Claud begins. 'They haven't got a right to put pressure on us this early. It's precisely why I wanted to keep a lid on things for as long as possible. To avoid this kind of hoopla.'

What she means is, Liz and Sam and no one else. He wants to shout at her simple-mindedness, this stupid, protectionist woman he has married.

'This is all rubbish as far as I'm concerned, 'Mal. Neither of us have any interest in God, for a start. We're a pair of healthy, rational atheists who wanted to get married in a great building. Same as everyone else our age.'

'Who said anything about raising him a Hindu? Didn't you hear them? One God, any God.'

'Read between the lines, Amal. Are you really that stupid? This is about you becoming a Christian. It's their way of getting back at me.'

'That's not true, Claud. Ma and Puppa aren't like that and you know it. It hacks me off that you even said it. They have no issue with me being baptized. If anything I think they're pleased that I'm actually showing an interest in religion.'

'Not theirs, though. They'd rather you followed theirs.'

She spoke like it was that easy; all that he had done. He had given up everything his parents taught him for three-quarters of an hour at a Victorian-built stone altar in Lewes.

Churches fly past at every half mile, as if to needle him

on what he has lost. For all the fuss, the importance made of it, they have not been inside one for worship since the wedding, Liz and Sam seemingly only interested in his membership, nothing more.

An adult christening is easy to fake. He could have said he got done on a quiet Tuesday afternoon at the Episcopalian place on Richmond Green, or the forbidding-looking Scottish Presbyterian house tucked away in Kew. He knew enough graphic designers to knock up a certificate, if one was needed. As it was, the vicar who joined them barely raised interest in the confirmation of his conversion, almost talked over it in fact, so keen was he to reach the part of the conversation that concerned fees.

It was an act on all their parts. There was no element of Christian teaching from his twelve evening sessions at a library room in Chiswick that resonated with him. No clear belief in the presence of Christ. Only a heightened awareness of the paraphernalia, and a new-found fascination for religious paintings, whether the gold-leafed Russian icons at the Victoria and Albert, or the gaudier, Hallmark-inspired depictions hung in the shops along Shepherd's Bush Road. He did it because it was the one thing she asked of him. Only after the wedding when his smug easiness lapsed into headache, similar to coming down from the most extreme sugar highs only more intense, did he see the folly of it, respecting his parents even more for not pointing it out.

Distance makes him a lousy son. He needs to be better, especially since he is about to become a father. Only . . .

Catholic, Methodist, Baptist, Anglican, First Adventist, and United Reformed architecture stand guard as he trips himself up, those good thoughts somehow leaving his brain and catching hard in his throat. Bunting streams from every lamp post as if to celebrate his amnesia. He can remember how one obscure B-road leads to the next, but not what has happened to their future child. It is pathetic how easily the collection of cells escaped him for those brief moments, like it was never there, seduced as he was by everything that makes the Sussex countryside so smart: the well-tended farmland, the villages with their lead into aspiration, and the essence of simple faith amplified by the collection of churches.

It must be a pang, an ache no deeper than a three-week crush. He feels better to think it away like this. Better than staring at a sleeping Claud, and wishing for the return of something that is no longer there. His crush on the supermodels as a teenager hurt more than this. He dry-humped the mattress imagining Cindy Crawford, Christy Turlington and Stephanie Seymour in the three months leading up to his exams. What is twenty-one days? How much can it mean, really?

He winds the window down a fraction to begin waking her. The breeze, gently pulling her out of her pill-induced sleep, has a lightness of touch he lacks; no heavier than fingertips removing a stray eyelash. She has ten miles to banish all that is groggy and incoherent. He was given a similar prescription last year when he pulled his knee at the gym. Knows the time it takes to lose the muddy speech and the feeling that the brain's pathways are connected by fuzzy felt.

But her face is not the blank canvas of a Mickey Finn. It is the countryside that has relaxed her; she is calmed by being in the world of Hawkhurst, Robertsbridge, and Burwash. His lack of presence in her history is coming to the fore, Sussex providing the comfort blanket he is unable to replicate. The day has been all about highlighting his deficiencies as a husband.

'Where are we?'

'Outside Battle. We'll be there before long.'

'I need to do my make-up. If they see me looking like this, they'll know something's up.'

'Get a quick cup of tea by the Abbey? I could do with shaking my lettuce.'

It is her first laugh, loud and warm, as if something in the combination of sleeping pill and countryside has lowered her barriers, made laughter a possibility. It cannot be because his jokes are funny; he comes from the cabaret school of bad gags. The car does not rock with mirth but pleasure somehow reaches both of them, flushing cheeks, suggesting a way to draw her out. Laughing will not make everything better, but it may make her stronger. It opens new avenues for his usefulness.

'I think you're bigging it up too much, 'Mal. It's not so much a lettuce, more a little gem.'

The abbey, rising at the far end of the high street, delivers an almost blasé sense of awe, as if the chintziness of the local stores has stripped it of its foreboding. It stands fully preserved and complete, unlike some of its cousins along the coast at Hastings and further east towards Kent. It has always been their gatepost, the final marking on the road home. Today, it is wrapped in ribbons of white bunting, as if to confirm that they have crossed the finish line. He wonders whether their future will always be tied to Sussex, spending their days fractious in plastic raincoats, still tiptoeing around what they really want to say.

They take an outside table at the tea shop overlooking the entrance where they can watch the trickle of silver tourists clutching their anoraks and guidebooks. The couples are predominantly women, murmuring agreeably in anticipation of one more landmark being crossed off their list. Aware of the statistics, he is still always surprised to see that it is more women than men happily taking the strain on the hill as they join the queue trailing from the admission booth. It is as if the threat of a late sentence stranded with their wives visiting empty spaces is too much to contemplate, has killed them off.

Pensioner is not a dirty word in their home. They have talked more about pension provision than they have about children because breeding is a given. It is one of the main points of getting married in their middle thirties; to use up the sperm and the eggs before they dry up, trail off, drop off. Financial planning for later life is not assumed in the same way, when other factors such as the stupidity of the husband are brought into account.

It came up on their first date, a forced meeting in a city bar arranged by Hari, who subsequently ditched them because he was so sure they would click. He cannot remember now what either of them was wearing, only her shoes, black patent Mary Janes, whose overt childishness was a marked contrast to her interrogating tone, somewhat Mary Poppins but with better lipstick.

'I read somewhere that first dates are essentially interviews with cocktails. Might as well go with that thought.'

'I thought we were just having a drink.'

'Shut up and answer the questions. Please confirm that you're in full-time employment, preferably something that is neither in the arts sector or a McJob.'

'I can indeed confirm that. Wouldn't you rather sit down, or is towering over me part of the "thing"?'

'I take it you're solvent?'

'Some of the time. I'm playing, don't take it so seriously, Claudia.'

'Claud. It's Claud. Just answer the questions. No ad-libs.'

'Sir! Yes sir!'

'Married? Attached?'

'No. No.'

'Have you joined a pension scheme or made adequate provision for pensionable age?'

'I have. It's buried under the bed.'

'Are you a homeowner?'

'Yes.'

'Close to your family?'

'Close enough. Do you want a top-up? Looks like you're running empty there.'

'Later. Any history of mental illness?'

'Only in agreeing to come out tonight.'

'Do you like being questioned by slightly scary women made even scarier by three cocktails on an empty stomach?'

'I love it. Give me more.'

She does not drink her latte until it is nearly cold. The milk has formed a thick skin whilst she works on her face, and when finally disturbed, it hangs off the side of the cup in a thick bandage, like rope, as she brings it to her lips. He takes it from her in a swift movement, both to draw her attention to the ugliness that adorns her glass, but also to stop him from gagging.

'Leave it. I can get you one fresh.'

'No need. It's just to wet the whistle. Couldn't have finished it anyway.'

'You wetting *your* whistle, me shaking my lettuce. We could go on tour with these phrases. Make a show out of it.'

She is not as amused as before. Though she has finished applying lipstick, her mouth stays fixed in a grimace, the mirror of him a minute ago when faced with crinkled, knotted milk skin. He stutters his way out of it.

'I-I-I-I'm hungry. Maybe I should get a sandwich or a cake.'

'Mum will have made lunch. She'll be offended if you don't make a go of it.'

'I'm eating for strength. I can't shift a washing machine on an empty stomach.'

'You don't need extra strength. Just use the bulk around your gut. Dad doesn't hold excess weight the way you do, otherwise he'd be on it himself.'

This is everything he has brought into the marriage: brawn over brain, and lacklustre sperm.

Her eyes, coloured on and around the lids, heavily coated with mascara, roam around their gatepost, as she cranes her head around his newly crowned bulk to settle upon the abbey.

'We used to hate it when we were kids. Thought it symbolized everything smug and bourgeois. There was a guy in sixth form who had this idea of burning it down on Christmas Eve.'

'What was the point of that?'

'To ruin Christmas for everyone. To get the TV cameras down here. Try and get on the news as an anxious bystander. We were attention-seeking buggers at that age. Real terrors.'

He has seen the picture albums and the home video footage, hours of it, but can still not imagine Claud as a child. He does not have the curiosity he has seen in other husbands because to him she has never been anything other than fully formed. So to think of her that way, formative and vulnerable, jars. Seeing her as she is now, damaged, unsure, takes him to the same place.

'B-bloody rich kids, Spoilt brats, the lot of you. What's with all the bunting, by the way? All the other villages we passed were decked out too.'

'Herald of spring, probably. Usually about this time of year. I'd forgotten all about it.'

She shudders, at the thought of any festival, pagan or otherwise, that celebrates fertility. The look in her eyes yearns for winter and the invisibility and numbness that comes with it.

'Do you think we can do this, 'Mal? I've never lied to my parents before.'

'I'm not calling the shots here. We'll do whatever you want. Whatever gets you through the day.'

'How do you lie? What can I say to make it sound convincing?'

'Like I'm the expert?'

'Men lie. It's in your DNA.'

'You do realize that I'm not like those guys. Where has this come from?'

'Don't get mad. I'm just having second thoughts.'

'You can do this, Claud. You just need some help. Keep it simple. Let them do the talking. If you can't keep it up, tell them.'

The waitress, like everyone they see in Battle, is unaware of their situation. So cheerfully ignorant that he wants to take it out on her, strangle her.

'Will be with you in a sec, my dears,' she calls after a hurried swish from tables to back counter, her second sight homing in on his hand as it trembles over the laminated menu card.

'This is why Rory wanted to torch the place. Reckoned it was making fogies out of us. Look at her, twenty years old and speaking like a granny.'

He cannot look at the waitress, past the pasty freckled hand as she grabs the menu post-order, and the sideways glance kitchenwards, alerting the staff that an Asian is on the premises; experience teaches him this, not self-indulged paranoia. He has no time to invest in her comings and goings, the way her back has stiffened, wary of possible complaint, sure of haggling over the bill and a withholding of the service charge. Ordinarily, these nuances would preoccupy him and ruin the snack. Today he is too busy looking at his wife.

She must have been an uncomplicated girl, the master of the universe even then. Other than growing pains she has had nothing to worry about. Her family has no history of serious illness. They have been good with their money. Her grandparents are still alive and living independently. The household pets, two overfed cats, were spared a descent into the indignity of old age after both were catnapped over two successive months. There has been no uncertainty in her life, nothing that has forced her to reflect. Try asking an Indian family what they have been spared and prepare for your ears to sting all the way back to the subcontinent as your jugs are pulled from your head.

He is not trying to rake up the cricket test again, India versus the UK, nor descend into who is better equipped to handle crises, white or brown. He attempts to ignore all that the Indian gene, smart and certain, wishes him to see. He is unable to understand her behaviour, how tears can be stopped so easily, and exploding abbeys discussed so casually. It is only as she talks of her teenage years, scarily textbook in her indie-gothic-fashioned angst, that he realizes how much he needs family around him, just not hers.

He remembers the fireworks between Ma and Puppa, arguments carrying on late into the night whenever he was late coming home from work; her back shaking with anger when meals were missed due to sudden card games or impromptu offers to fix friends' cars. He remembers furniture upturned, and plates being smashed, each struggling to grab hold of the other's throat, one to pacify, the other to exterminate. What he and Claud have is all that he wished for – the opposite of his parents; all comfort and no spark. Everything about their life is mild-mannered, even their arguments. Rowing dispensed no differently than their vitamins, succinctly, and at the allotted hour.

When he arrives home in the early hours, acting like Puppa, she understands that it is at the behest of Hari. There is a grunt of recognition that he has returned before she rolls over to continue sleep. No, where have you been, shitty arse, as Ma greeted drunk, befuddled, pleased with himself Puppa.

This is the time to reject simplicity in the face of loss. No more grey, just black and white. Black or White. He wants tears from her, anger, blame. He would rather she laid it all on his door, his taking the eye off the ball, for being so inept in his caring for her, for lacking medical skills and not committing to the required background reading from the moment the test showed positive. He cannot accept all this sitting around and eating cake, even though it was his suggestion. He is ready to hear how he left it all to her.

Instead, he lashes out at the waitress for bringing dry, stale sponge, not as advertised, and the sandwich on a damp plate which has made the bread soggy and inedible.

'I'm sorry, but you're having a laugh if you think this is professional catering. Both these plates are an absolute joke. Your next attempt needs to be better than this if you stand any chance of getting the bill paid.'

The waitress's shoulders finally relax, enjoying the marked rise in his tone, which is making the other customers shake their teacups nervously, relieved that what she has been waiting for has finally arrived.

''Mal, don't.'

'What d'you mean, don't? Is this acceptable food? Are you happy paying seven pounds for this?'

'This is the way we serve food down here, my dear. No other person has complained about so-called stale cakes to my knowledge. So if you don't like it, I suggest you clear off.'

He hears Claud talking to him in a low, vehement tone but does not respond, feeling his genomes putting every single cell into a chokehold. The untutored Indian gene has been allowed to grow rotten within him, ready to fight hostility with hostility. He is ever alert for signs of discord in the day-to-day world, willing to pounce upon sources of hate with their upturned lips and sloppy service until they are ripped to shreds. Others are evolved and can look past milk skin and stale cake, but not him, Neanderthal in his emotional drive. When he suddenly stands up and pushes the offending plates towards the waitress's face, he acts on impulses that cannot be de-programmed. He is a genetic warrior. He will fight to the death to remove all unwanted aggression.

When the row is taken indoors, to the kitchen entrance away from the bulk of customers, he is fired-up and feels more alive than he has been all day, alert and ready for a show of strength. The manager is a thin-lipped southern European with a thick carb-fed gut who only wants to diffuse the situation. He looks at the waitress like she is a liability, not needing to hear from any witnesses that she was the first person to start swearing. He only has to look at Amal, arguing to the point of tears, as if every fibre of his being is backing him up. He wants to fight now cry later, but one does not come without the other. In the privacy of the kitchen, away from a waiting Claud, the manager and lippy waitress watch a grown man fall to pieces over two-day-old cake. The bill is waived.

⁂

A dog is crapping outside the gift shop. Its owner, an old girl with thick round sunglasses, tells him to fuck off when he asks her to pick up the mess.

'Mind your own business,' she says. 'I don't tell you how to do things in your country.'

Claud is looking for something else for Liz. The tartan blankets have been discarded.

'They'll have to go in the next charity collection. Why

did you let me buy that tat? That's how they get you, the service stations, luring you with their combinations of pretty displays and bad lighting.'

'Is Liz really going to appreciate a Battle tea towel? She'll have hundreds. We should get going, shouldn't we?'

'Just wait a minute, Amal. I know you're still hot and bothered from the café, and want to get out of here, but you'll have to wait. I need something for my mother.'

'We resolved everything, actually. I'm not worried about being stoned out of town.'

'Your face is red.'

'It was one of those professional kitchens. You know how hot they get.'

Claud's face is reddish too; a combined disgust with both him and her defunct motorway purchase. The flush is a good thing, means that her blood is running through her, means strength, although he does not feel that she will welcome the news. Strength equals getting better equals back to normal: mid-thirties, childless, living in a soulless house.

She takes to a corner that holds the local art; jugs and pots, polka-dotted and looking falsely nautical in their blues, whites, and greens. His time in Battle so far does not share the same bucolic peace advertised by these rough and ready crafts. He cannot help thinking that each flask, tile or pot should have a nail driven through it, or a painted missive saying FROGS OUT, WOGS OUT.

He is being oversensitive, and a prick; a troublemaker, looking to make ignorant, peaceful lives rattled and unpleasant. He cannot help it. His back is up, hooked like a junkie in the way his chest has been thumping, hard and sharp, ever since he was asked to follow the young fogey waitress down the back to settle his complaint.

Even in the thick of it, his ears drumming with a sense of insult, he was aware of how the girl's lips glistened with stray saliva every time she harrumphed in indignation. The wetness of them, as they pursed out, back and forth, surprisingly full and thick, leading to thoughts of what she looked like out of her food-stained tabard, whether he could screw the hate out of her like he'd done with other girls in his bachelor past.

He is a disgusting pig, a disgrace, but this feeling something, a deep loathing, lust, is unshakeable and continues to power him. He is alive. These sick perversions confirm it.

There is also a new animation in Claud. Not to say that the act of shopping has awoken something in her, but some aspect of it has played its part, along with the gritty undrinkable milk skin and the sense of purpose in finding something that will surprise and give pleasure to Liz. Maternal approval: a daughter's greatest battery charger. He should have realized it. There is nothing that a mother's love is not capable of untangling and putting right.

She wants one of two paintings that hang on the wall: close oil studies of the castle rock on largish canvases. The thick, crumbly brick packed tightly around a windowless turret shows how time erodes greater than man-made pollutants, appearing on the precipice of decay. But it has been painted pleasingly for tourists, playing with gold dusk light, referring to an unedifying presence, and a vague promise of morning renewal, like the bar drunk's motto: everything will be all right tomorrow. The painting is untitled but this is what it should be.

He understands why it makes a good gift for Liz, and recognizes the space on the stair wall where it should hang as Claud describes it. What he cannot make sense of is the stillness he feels as he looks at it. The sensation of his temper slowly diffusing into the brick, absorbed by centuries of stoicism like a stone shock protector, until the heaviness in his upper chest and around his neck dissipates and finally is no longer there.

They should be giving something more alive, not this dead thing that has drained all his bad impulses. Is this how it will be from now on, presenting dead gifts, stone, metal, abstract, when previously they looked for flowers, plants, and other items designed to warm the soul rather than extinguish it?

Claud stands on a footstool and half-pulls half-lifts the canvas from the wall, grunting with effort as if she is taking a slab of castle stone with her. The canvas itself is cheaply backed with balsa, light but cumbersome. Even still, something like panic lodges in his throat. She should not be doing this.

'Here. Let me.'

'Get off, 'Mal. I'm fine. Not an invalid yet.'

They grapple unsurely for a moment, each stubborn to the wishes of the other, standing at either end of the now unhooked canvas fighting for space in the cramped shop – two squabbling removal men. Laurel and Hardy or Morecombe and Wise.

'Let go, I said! You're going to knock things over the way you're carrying on.'

'I'm only trying to help.'

'Stop mollycoddling me. I don't need wrapping up in cotton wool. How many times!'

Her make-up, all four products of it – powder, lipstick, mascara and blush – have made a warrior of her. They are tired of each other, this dance of stepping lightly running its course, now speaking in their office voices, bossy, impersonal and untouched by tragedy. Everyone in the shop has heard.

'Why did you discharge yourself before I got a chance to speak to the doctor?'

He realizes he is still angry from the café. Nothing in these pastoral arts and crafts or this crappy painting has sedated him. Each wonky piece needles him to the point where it feels like he is lying on a bed of nails. That she is clutching the canvas so tightly, the way he imagines a mother's hand suctioned onto a toddler's makes him hate it even more.

'You want to talk about this here?'

'Why not? You've already told them that I'm suffocating you, pretty much. I didn't realize that a man looking out for his wife could be so mortally offensive.'

'It was a busy day for admissions. I told you.'

'I'm sorry. I just find it hard to believe that they would turf you out on the street before the agreed time, and before a family member arrived. Look at the state of you. Hardly in a fit state to be wandering the hospital left alone.'

'I've had a miscarriage. I'm not a mental patient.'

It is the first time she's said it. The word clangs around the pottery and metalwork, unclaimed, ringing uncomfortably to nosy ears. Still he is too caught up in his tirade to mark the event, see progress. He only wants to rip the canvas from her and bind her hands so that she is incapable of lifting anything else until she is better.

'They shouldn't have let you go without seeing me first. They should have seen us together. It was out of order not to.'

She too speaks quickly, as if talking over him will erase the word, and bring about a collective amnesia. It was a slip of the tongue, not a breakthrough.

'This is the NHS, 'Mal, where the world doesn't revolve

around our little problem. We're minnows compared to the disease around us. They did what they needed to do. Now it's your turn.'

Because everything is about his job, his role in their marriage. He struggles to pinpoint what it is she actually does in theirs, what she brings to the table aside from the born-right of her gender to have the last word.

'You have to take an interest all the time, not just when I'm pregnant.'

Her accusatory tone forces him into this behaviour. Similar circumstances dictated the late nights at the office or elsewhere during those months when they were supposed to be conceiving. When she spoke and acted like that, unimpressed and dissatisfied with his effort, ready to take him apart with sarcasm, he wanted to be away from her. And for the most part he managed it, dutifully fucking her in the morning when she had reached her optimal internal temperature, necking his pro-biotic and then disappearing to work.

He knows how this will pan out. When she has recovered her strength, and her tongue, he will be blamed. Neglect of conjugal duties has lost their collection of cells. Staying out late has done this. Lying. He has not paid enough attention to her, has used the wrong detergent on the clothes, has kissed her with warm shellfish breath. If it does not come from her it will fire from Liz and Sam, or even Ma and Puppa. He is the husband. He is not there to be exonerated. It is in the contract.

She walks out of the shop with the tunnel-vision of a shoplifter. It is left to him to get his card out. The woman at the counter gives him the receipt, a roll of bubble-wrap, and a look of last rites.

Outside, catching her, a brisk few paces which makes him breathless, she refuses his offer of help, walking ahead of him all the way.

'Leave me alone.'

He does not even try to catch up. It hurt, how her words took physical shape in the air as they were spat out. Part of him hopes she will trip or drop the thing, just so he can be turned to for help, and proved right.

The BMW is a useless piece of tin crap, squeezing them together in a way that they do not wish to be squeezed. It is a car for couples hooked on contact, who would find roominess in a well or in certain styles of fucking. Common-laws in love, who only feel complete when skin is glued on skin, permeable and permanent.

Both his car and the Mini Cooper were bought in this spirit, when unions were only ever thought to be happy and unbreakable. Now they need something bigger; a four seater, long and wide. A tank, like the Mercedes S Class, where she can sit at the back and sulk with the painting propped beside her, and he can be left alone, putting his foot down on the series of undulating hills that trail to Lewes.

The best she can do is wedge the now bubble-wrapped

painting between them. From gear stick to ceiling, they are cut off from each other with this mobile Berlin Wall. Only the closeness of the other's breath, and their scent, can pass through and over flimsy plastic wrap. They cannot see but they can hear: fits and snorts and odd exclamations removed from all recognizable language.

He hopes that speed will help, that the faster he goes, the quicker their clouds can be shaken off. He is not angry with her, only with himself, suffocating in remorse as thick and impenetrable as the bubble-wrap. His head feels as if it is filled with tiny negative bubbles which need to be popped one by one. Does not listen. Pop. Childish. Pop. Ignorant with no concept of art. Pop. Defective sperm. Pop. Bad choice of husband. Pop. He does not hear her voice until she is in full flow. She is talking on the phone, using his mobile, which lies charging on her side.

'I've got Hari waiting on the line, 'Mal. I think you have something to tell him.'

In his readiness to make allowances, to mourn, he has forgotten what a bitch she can be. If things are not to her liking he will be cut dead guaranteed, from arguing over their choice of supermarket when they first moved in together, to her insistence of being fucked in a yoga position, irrespective of his pleasure, because according to all the literature, it was the best way to conceive. She has this need to be in control of every element or at least to have a well-argued say. Even weather reports are not believed if they do not fall into the scheme of things. It will definitely not rain because it is warm enough for bare legs; there needs to be at least five centimetres of snow because what is the point of spending exorbitantly on getting three pairs of custom-made Uggs shipped over from New Zealand if they cannot be worn before the end of March?

But phoning Hari is the lowest she has ever sunk, making him feel like a naughty school kid being slapped across the legs for misbehaviour. School ma'am knows best. He hates everything about her slyness, this compulsion she has to put him on the spot.

Hari is with him, not finding it funny as she does.

'What's happened? I don't understand what's going on.'

'That makes two of us.'

'She said there was bad news. Have things gotten worse?'

'Not quite.'

'You don't sound like you're in the hospital, more like a car. Is it an ambulance? Is she being transferred? I heard that some women bleed to death, but not in a hospital surely?'

Hari's voice rises with excitement at the prospect of being so close to crisis. Amal pictures his face, consummately metrosexual, expectant, and ready to shoot his load if the details are particularly delicious and nasty. Probably holding a pen in readiness so as not to miss a thing, or speed-dialling on a second phone to reach Ma and Puppa. Even in the tensest moment he can only find this behaviour endearing, worthy of a punch on the arm or a drunken kiss on the forehead. How can he forgive his friend, lurching on the precipice of gossip, and not his own wife? What does that say about his divided loyalties?

'We've had a nasty shock, Hari. You should probably sit down.'

The news he is expected to deliver sticks in his throat, and not just because she is monitoring his every nuance or because he has never been so aware of how comfortable he is with lying, and telling people what they most want to hear. It feels like they are playing with the collection of cells. Pissing on its watery grave. How does indulging in these petty mind games make things any better? None of their behaviour features in the recommended pamphlets on grieving. He hears the sharp intake of breath from the other side of the partition, which tells him that she is not ready to exhale until he has spoken just the way she wants him to. She would probably write cue cards if the painting was not in the way.

'But I know this already,' Hari says, after he has demeaned himself with this two-way pretence. 'Why are you telling me again?'

'As one of our closest friends we wanted you to be the first to be told. We're on our way to Sussex now to break it to Liz and Sam.'

'I get it. She doesn't know you called me last night, does she? You're acting like you're scared of her, Amal. This is not the action of a strong Indian husband.'

'It's not a question of that. We just wanted you to know.'

'All right! I get the message. You're spineless and unable to stand up to your wife. Kid had a lucky escape if you ask me.'

Amal swallows this because he is not prepared to make him look bad in front of Claud. It would be easy payback, putting Hari on speaker and letting him twist the knife, but he does not have the stomach for it. Privately, he will kick the shit out of him at a later date, but not now. Now is the time for murmured platitudes, sweetness and light.

'See? I knew you'd feel better if you got it off your chest,' says Claud, satisfied, once he hangs up, not understanding that the break in his chest is one of frustration and has nothing to do with her.

'Better out than in.'

It kills him to stay calm, keeping his breathing as smooth as the engine, resisting all urges to push her out, smash them into a tree.

'You keep too many things to yourself, 'Mal. I could see what it was doing to you in the shop. You looked like you were going to fall apart.'

'That was hunger pangs from not eating the sandwich.'

'Stop running away from it. Be brave enough to face it.'

Says the girl who has shoved a canvas between them. Who cannot look him in the face after losing his baby. She should be taken to court for what she did. If she was poor and uneducated she probably would be.

'We're nearly there. Five minutes.'

'We can pull up at the next lay-by if you want a cry.'

'I don't want or need a cry, Claud. I'm fine.'

He is not worried about tears, only the double and triple knots that have made a cat's cradle of his guts; wrenched tightly, as if his emotions are on a leash. He wonders whether they will look back and see this as a turning point, when it began to physically hurt to share the same space. Neither Claud's stabs nor Hari's bleating distract from this. The car purrs as smoothly as ever but everything within it sits wrong.

She feels something too. Thumps on the dashboard to convey it. The canvas prevents him from seeing the degree of unease etched on her face. He only has the urgency of the thumps to guide him: a series of double raps becoming louder and more frequent the further he drives, until what was first a signal morphs into a drum beat; jungle drums, communicating the depth of their contrition. He hears the un-clunk of the seat beat holder, indicating she is ready to spring into action the moment he stops the car.

At the next lay-by, where a young couple are trading

cellophane-wrapped roses, she sprints towards the privacy of the furthest verge and dry heaves. That she wants to purge the poison so physically, the rot that has accumulated since their arrival in Battle, makes him go soft. His chest cavity rises and falls as a series of emotional waves breaks the marital surf. Her retching is synchronicity, proof that a connection exists, but he is still too pig-headed to show it.

'See! I told you this is what would happen if you drank that manky coffee!'

⁓

'Right, I thought, I'm not standing for this. So I went to the printers in the marketplace, the French chap, you know, where we did your wedding invites, and got five thousand of my own printed up.'

'Fighting fire with fire? You're a braver man than I am, Sam.'

'Protect Lewes, it says. End the bureaucratic madness now! Cost an arm and a leg because we went with a heavier card to stand out more, but it's worth it. Here, see?'

'"Let's nip it in the bud." Very catchy.'

'Mention red tape round here and it's like a rallying cry.'

'So I see. "Red or white, let's unite and fight." Sounds like you're recruiting for the Spanish Civil war, or something. Never had you down as the communist type.'

'People won't put up with the nonsense you see

happening in other towns. Look what's happened to Ashford, and Dover. Can't take a piss without government bodies having their say.'

'Sounds like a lot of effort for something that's still a proposal. They haven't even held the public consultation yet, have they?'

'You have to catch them on the hop, Amal. Be prepared before they are. Why would you want to put an asylum tribunal centre into the Cedars? Ruin a perfectly good house when they could easily use an unused tower block in the city. We're in the middle of the country. We have nothing for them here, these people.'

'They probably need something close to the coast, I suppose. Scouring round for something local.'

'Then set up in Dover! Don't ruin our lovely town! They should be hunting in busier places like Hastings or Brighton. If you have a train, you take it to the train station, not the motorway. This kind of rubbish is a drain on our local facilities.'

'You've written that over sixty per cent of those who make it through the tunnel from France illegally end up in a spiral of crime and prostitution. Where are you getting these figures from?'

'It's an estimate. Just to give people a rough idea.'

'Nothing like scaremongering to get them going, eh?'

'Sod 'em. I don't have to explain myself to anybody. I'm a private citizen having his own say.'

'Just be careful you're not misleading people, Sam. You could get pulled up for stuff like this.'

'Let them try. Do you read the papers where you are? They're at war all along the South coast, and I don't want it brought here. I have my grandchild to think about. I don't want little Claud or baby Amal not being able to walk to the park because there's drug dealers and brothels at every corner.'

'So the grandchild's to blame, is it?'

'I'm thinking about the future. It's what you do when you get to my age. Pass us that coaster, will you? Liz'll have me strung up by the balls if I get a wet mark on the new sofa. We haven't scotch-guarded yet.'

Things are done the old-fashioned way in Lewes. Mother and daughter commandeer the kitchen whilst Amal is left to attend his father-in-law in the lounge. Male company, even the watered-down type that Amal offers, is welcome, but what Sam wants most of all is for his daughter to be with him. His notices how his father-in-law's eyes betray that sentiment every time he speaks, flickering towards the door expectantly. Every time he hugs her – hello and goodbye – he clamps onto her like he is wielding a vice. His prized girl, missing for seven days and now back. Amal too is hugged, but the outpouring of love on the drive is reserved only for her. Liz by contrast is breezy and peckish with her kisses, almost embarrassed by Sam's display, uncomfortably long and silent, oblivious to all onlookers.

Amal too looks at the door in the direction of the kitchen and wills the intrusion of feminine company, the opposite of his desires at home. He kids himself that it is in Claud's best interests; to rescue her from Liz's pregnancy talk. Comparing notes on a baby that does not exist. But there is something that holds him back, stops him from getting up and joining them at the breakfast bar, whether under the pretext of refilling the coffee cup or looking for biscuits. He is relieved not to have to hear her lying about the supposed bump growing inside her. Thankful he does not have to be party to her fake optimism. His sanguinity is hard enough to maintain, here, in this casual setting that still feels like an extended interview, three years after the main event.

He never wants that specific tone to reach his ears, her fraudulent hopefulness, because he knows that he will always be looking out for it from then on. Mulling over every aspect of their marriage and reliving the moments when she talked to him in the same way, from reworking a route after the SatNav went bust, to nights in bed when they wanted to try new things before conception bogged them down and made them weary, humping machines, well-dressed sperm and egg-holders.

Forcing themselves to pretend to Liz and Sam is a one-off. It has to be. Once things return to normal there will be no other reason to lie.

Sam nods towards the leaflet, expecting more praise

about the thick card, better suited to an invitation than a flyer handed out during market day. Bloody awful. Calligraphy-font gilt edging, with an art direction that lends itself better to an advertisement for curtain makers. The Frenchman must have seen him coming.

He knows what comes next, strains of pondering aloud that will rope him into being a glorified paperboy. Spending the afternoon with Sam on the Green, taking advantage of the numbers drawn by the Herald of Spring fair, with its stalls and tombola and mini bouncy castle. Supper will be sung for, and he will be made to campaign hard before transplanting the fight over to Richmond, bending the ears of every affluently conscious juicer and latte sipper, where every sentence ends with 'not on my doorstep'.

He resists the dogsbody role at every opportunity, but knows this is all part of the son-in-law's contract, to act the servile, agreeable chaiwalla. Whilst other men, those English Lionhearts that chased Claud so persistently in her teens and early twenties, would have embraced the role, he wonders what it is that makes him resist – the rebelliousness in his own nature, or the taken-for-granted way that Sam speaks to him, like a more arrogant Puppa, as if there are no options but his.

'Don't you want to get started on the washing machine? I heard it was urgent.'

'Sit down, mate. There's plenty of time for that. Liz's getting a spread sorted. We'll have a bash at it afterwards. You're always in such a hurry, Amal.'

'Am I?'

'You are. Being industrious is in your DNA I suppose. You can't build an Empire without it.'

'Rebuild an Empire, you mean.'

'I was just making an observation, not getting political.'

He cannot be angry when Sam has his hands raised in surrender, sheepish at the slip of his tongue; though the underlying aura is one of satisfaction, as if his father-in-law is secretly pleased with himself for speaking his mind. No different to the intent of the leaflets: rant now, apologize later.

Every weekend visit encompasses much of the same. Last Saturday, he was grilled over his thoughts on education, whether the schools in Richmond could compete with the combination of high academic standards and pastoral care offered by the triumvirate of prep schools in the surrounding villages; the assumption being that Sussex was the only viable place to bring up a child. Now the focus is on the safety of the environment, and of Sam's one-man effort to force out all that is pestilent and unsavoury. These debates are set to continue until a baby is held securely in a grandfather's arms – until the next issue comes along needing to be worried about.

In the three weeks since the news, both Liz and Sam appeared to have undergone two contradictory procedures: they are invigorated, and yet they look older – old – as if something in Claud's teasing question 'are you ready to be grandparents?' has triggered conflict within their bodies.

Their molecular structure has been waiting all this time for an alarm call, and now that it has been triggered, their physiognomy has accelerated them into their third age. His eyes are bright, but the face appears more deeply lined; tufts of hair sprouting from ears and eyebrows look unrulier than before. The hairline itself has further receded, making the sharp side parting look as though it springs as far back as his crown, and the skin across hands and elbows appears looser, although the efforts of the tanning bed do their best to cover it. Most obvious of all is the slackening in his posture, from the curve in his lower back, making his belly protrude, to the newly risen hunch at the base of his neck.

Dad to Grandad in twenty-one days. It is irreversible. Now they have committed so wholeheartedly, their middle-age can only be viewed as past. Grandparents without a grandchild. He and Claud are still capable of any transformation, but Sam, and by extension Liz, Ma and Puppa too, will remain this old, waiting for a child's birth to power them.

Only the secondary development, this new-found energy, will save them; a deep-rooted motor that has given them purpose, battling the ravages of cellular decay. They cannot be protected from heartache, grief for something so small they cannot even put a fitting name to it. But this rediscovered energy will rally them into positive thinking, pushing them back into the thrust of harebrained schemes such as the opposing of the asylum tribunal centre. Amal hopes that he and Claud can be swept up in the whirlwind. They need these arms around them.

When female company arrives it is not in the numbers they were hoping for. There is only one of them. Amal fiddles with the flyer, glad that he still has it in his hand, hoping that Liz does not register the disappointment on both his and Sam's faces. She is carrying a tray loaded with food, and though she is concentrating on not spilling anything, the flickering in her eyes registers their dissatisfaction, that she is only second billing to the main show in spite of her careful clothing choices, dark jeans and a short white shirt folded at the sleeves, and light make-up. He thinks of how Ma would feel if she were treated the same way and his ears burn with uncensored shame. He only realizes now how Claud is the centre of the house. Everything else is periphery.

'I was going to set things up in the dining room, but since there's just the three of us, there's no point, really. We can just eat off our laps.'

Panic casts across Sam's face, sharply nipped in the bud by his wife. Familiarity with his impulses. Revenge.

'She's lying down upstairs. Had a rough night, she said. And I think she was still feeling nauseous from the car.'

'Been tearing down the B roads have you, Amal? Not looking after my daughter?'

'Quite the opposite, Sam. It's why it's taken us so long to get down here.'

'It's nothing to do with speed, Samuel. Her body's all over the place. The smell of a freshly laundered cotton towel could make her feel sick just as much as a car journey. Remember how I was when I was carrying her?'

Lunch is the deli counter's finest decanted into bowls and layered on plates. Aside from the baguette still warm from the oven everything is cold: slices of ham and cheese, boiled eggs, leaf and roasted vegetable salads, and jar upon jar of condiments. There is a leg of lamb in the fridge ready to be roasted should they be persuaded to stay for dinner, but before five in the afternoon Liz makes it a rule to spend as little time as possible on the stove. Life is too short.

Ordinarily, Amal would be playfully whispering to Claud about his yearning for a hot dog or a Pot Noodle over this picnic food, how he would welcome any crap so long as it was hot. Now he silently tucks in, surprising himself by how hungry he actually is. He is free to put it away, singularly focusing on his appetite and forgetting about Claud whilst she sleeps. If Liz and Sam are sharing the same thoughts they do not show it. Emotion is difficult to gauge when the subjects of observation are tugging on French sticks with Polydented teeth. The room is silent save for slurping, gnawing and the scraping of cutlery against porcelain. They are finally comfortable with each other's company, now that food has filled the spaces they struggle to inhabit with words.

'Has he been showing you those ridiculous flyers? He was supposed to be taking me to Bruges on the Eurostar next month, but he's the blown the cash on those things.'

'They'll stand out, that's for sure.'

'Hand those out in the street and people will think they're being invited to a posh party somewhere. And then they read it . . .'

'That was the point, darling. Element of surprise. Fool them into a false sense of security and then nab 'em.'

'You can't hand those out in the street, Samuel. People will think you've gone mad.'

'And I should do it your way, I suppose. Sit on my backside and let every petty criminal and scrounger flood into our town.'

'Don't get clever. You might start choking on an olive. Good printer though, Amal. We've used him for a few things now.'

'She's only saying that because she fancies him.'

'Who wouldn't? Unattached, good-looking Frenchman in his thirties. He's a dish.'

'You're making a fool of yourself, Liz.'

'Half the women in the village are nutty for him. Claud would see the potential if she bumped into him.'

'Is that so, dear?'

'Don't make it sound sordid, Samuel. I'm just trying to explain how we share the same taste in men.'

'Because me and Amal are so much alike?'

'I was thinking more along the lines of how we both used to like George Michael. Stop teasing the boy, and eat your baguette. Amal, you don't have to go leafleting with him. You're under no obligation. He'll be bored of it himself by next week.'

'They're flyers, woman. Nothing is being sacrificed.'

'Just my weekend in Bruges.'

So it is confirmed. He is expected to go canvassing today, before lunch has even settled, the washing machine was simply a front to get them down here. He has fallen for carrots before, the docile working animal that he is, but never something as cumbersome and potentially hernia-giving as this.

'Is that before or after we shift the washing machine? I'm ready to put my power belt on.'

Sam grapples with a pickled onion and plays dumb. It is left to Liz to put down her sandwich and enlighten him.

'Don't worry about that now, Amal. I managed to get him to open that tight little wallet of his. Someone from the shop's coming on Tuesday to plumb it in. Didn't he tell you?'

When he goes to check on Claud before walking down to the village with Sam he finds her curled under a blanket but awake. Her face has softened in her old bedroom. Nothing can trouble her here.

'They keep sticking their head round the door. Every time I think I'm about to go off I hear those bloody creaky hinges.'

'Your dad has a new project. I'm going canvassing.'

'Mum was telling me. Take them both, will you? Get them out of my hair.'

'What'll you do?'

'Sleep. Maybe pick at some food. Just fancy some space.'

When she looks at him with that face he cannot deny her anything: marriage, a house that was too expensive for them, a kid.

'Sure. Anything.'

They are a ten-minute walk from the village, the house tucked into the base of a hill that gives rise to the Downs Way. There should be something oppressive about the valley-like surroundings, where neither man nor concrete structure can tower over nature, but sheltered by rolling chalk uplands, gnarled oaks and thick, wild hedgerows it is pleasing to urban eyes and makes a fine, if challenging walk to the pub at the top end of the Green. Unlike his trail leaders he feels the surge of heat across his cheeks and a dry, stinging breathlessness after the first few hundred yards uphill.

He is struggling with the Battle canvas which Liz is donating to the tombola. She decided it was eligible less than ten seconds after it was presented.

'Darling, it's lovely, but would you mind terribly if I donate it to the Herald? They've been at me for weeks and the only other thing I could think of is the pasta machine.'

He is carthorse for father as well as mother. Not only does the canvas's height hamper his vision, but the bulk and weight from the stack of leaflets shoved into his jacket and back packet ensure the inflexibility of every step.

Though he knows the terrain by heart – there have been many of these walks with either one or both in-laws since before the engagement; Ma and Puppa even struggling up the hill twice during the wedding rehearsal week – he realizes that he has arrived at the village parade when the stream of bunting begins. More rows of the same white ribbons that have marked their journey from the A-road are wantonly doubled over, like silly string, and trail the main road and footpath that lead to the Green, making those final few steps feel like being led to the Wizard of Oz.

It only occurs to him now that both Liz and Sam are wearing white shirts and shoes, and there are other white-shirted figures busying themselves along the Green with the opening business of the Herald of Spring afternoon. It is the unofficial uniform for every Pagan festival celebrated in twenty-first century England, especially this one, where the soberness of winter's dying days, its loathed browns and blacks, are finally shaken off. Colour is welcome but white is all right.

'We could do this another time. I thought you'd want to listen to the cricket.'

'Nothing worth hanging around for. They're getting slaughtered. I'll catch up with it later.'

'Our poor son. Are you flagging so soon?'

Liz has a chuckle at his expense, expecting to be joined in, but with Sam forging ahead her laugh is absorbed by hedgerows that flank the road. They all know him as a spectator, unwilling to take part in overtly physical activity. When the midsummer charity tug of war took place on the Green to raise funds for the village hall he stayed at the back hoping to keep out of trouble, not realizing that those who held on to the last fringes of rope had to exert themselves even more than the rest. He almost gave himself a hernia with the muscular pull he had to draw from the benign fullness of his soft, wobbly stomach, and when that failed, his guts. Similarly, on a family weekend on the Scilly Isles he had been unwilling to play racket ball with Sam, wary of a descent into competition, almost having a bat forcibly thrust into his hand by Claud to avoid argument.

'Play the damn game, 'Mal. Stop throwing a spanner every five minutes.'

The family, his new family, cannot accept that he is not a physical person. He has been raised on food and books and the need to find a secure career. In Leicester they are not outdoors people, all of life's learning comes from within the home.

By the time he reaches the Green with Liz, he sees leaflets in several hands. Sam is impatient to get his message across, covering ground with an attacking speed. Amal wonders how effective a few flyers thrust into the same circle of people day after day actually is. Whether they will end up as beer mats and non-absorbent pooper scoopers by the end of the afternoon.

'Let him have his fun,' says Liz, reading his mind.

Being married to the same person for almost thirty-six years does that, he supposes, makes you apologetic on your husband's behalf, understanding that others are not predisposed to show the same level of tolerance to a man's projects. He wonders whether Claud is already doing the same for him, if this is an intuition all wives take possession of on their wedding day along with the compliments and the treasure on the wedding list.

They head towards the tombola to deposit the canvas, whose wretched weight pulls without mercy on his upper arms and tightens in spasm across his knuckle joints. If he had been on his own he would have made at least three or four rest stops en route, but he has clung on regardless, conscious that Liz should not have any cause to believe that her daughter married a sissy. When he finally dumps it on the prize table, currying favour with some tired-looking soft toys, cheap local wine, and an unimpressive fruit basket, he slams it down harder than he intends to; the clunk of the wooden frame against the flimsy trestle table amplifying his intention to never see the damn painting again.

Free to roam, the pair of them watch as Sam holds court with a group of men in their late forties and early fifties with whom the leaflets generate close discussion. As if to make up for lost time he already has a pint in hand.

'He's been like this since he retired. All this is a wild goose chase of course, but it gives him a reason to get up in the mornings. It'll stop once the baby arrives.'

So it is not just true of him and Claud. Everyone around them is using their due date to put an end to their personal issues. They are all after a clean slate.

'I've seen men not dissimilar to him on those morning talk shows. They're a bunch of windbags,' he says lightly, a return joke for the knocking of his poor athleticism. What he holds back from describing is the demented self-belief of some of those men.

He overdosed on too much daytime TV last year recovering from the busted knee and grew familiar with the breed. It feels like the male response to empty nest syndrome – men overtaken with their singular campaigning, consumed with it to the point where family become the casualty. Obsessed with kicking out kerb crawlers, eastern bloc immigrants, the building of new mosques in residential areas, teenage anti-social behaviour, and plastic bottle recycling plants, they end up pushing away all that they seek to protect.

Liz always has a stoic look about her, able to take any amount of his nonsense. He cannot speak for Claud, but recognizes how she encourages her father's childishness, precisely because it too makes her feel young, and safe. A girl and her dad. Whilst he and Liz regularly roll their eyes at Sam's suggestions, she is the first to volunteer for dry tobogganing down the hill or an impromptu cycle race around the village. Father and daughter are more alike than they realize.

Amal hates everything about the campaigning zeal bar that it gets Sam off his back. There is something lonely in the man with the stiff posture as he walks from group to group clutching his empty pint glass, something like the beggars he despises. It makes a sad sight, and he is surprised about how protective he feels towards him, so much so that he almost quickens his pace to join him and put him at his ease, if it was not such bad manners to leave Liz alone.

He is plied with tea and cake from one of the stalls. The

village is not one of the ecologically aware, bohemian ones further away from the coast attracting the disillusioned city dwellers. The population here is more workaday, and ageing. Therefore he gets the special treatment and the nice china, being 'from London', a euphemism designed to cover a sea of other observations. He is called 'London lad' when warmly greeted by a couple of the older men, which manages to both flatter and insult in its delivery. There are children everywhere all of whom he tries to ignore. It is not the sight of them, mostly chubby and boisterous, more their sound that seems to force the shutters down deep within his chest. The idea of welcoming childish joy on this day would cripple him. Already their laughter acts as a mummifying agent, like formaldehyde, killing all sensation in his arms and legs. He looks at them critically, shaking his head at each heckle and squabble. His children would be raised better than this sorry lot. His children would behave and know their place.

The post on the Green trails white ribbon, purely decorative, unlike the hardier string they use on May Day and Midsummer's Eve. Unable to believe his eyes, he ragged Claud endlessly when he first saw it, like an East Midlands hick who had little experience of the world outside the city.

'Your parents live in a village where there's Morris dancing? Exactly what kind of place have you brought me to?'

Even though no one dances beneath it, the children too taken with their violent revolution aboard the bouncy castle and at the water rifle range where parents are repeatedly shot for the simple misdemeanour of refusal, the adults converging around the trestle table outside the pub on which lies a spread of cakes and ale, he still feels uncomfortable to be near it; something in the back of his mind telling him he would be tied to it if he comes any closer than five feet. The post is primal and brutal, used for celebration as well as punishment. Standing within its radius, not tethered, makes him a shorter King Kong, unleashed, free to pillage stores and ravage local women.

He is glad he held back from shaving, because the two-day growth, what they will suspiciously label as a beard, helps the cause enormously. Makes him look like a brown-skinned bogeyman, alien to the tea and scones, the fair-weather skin, and once round the maypole, merrily merrily.

But they are not like that with him, expelling his crass paranoia within minutes. Firstly, everyone offers their congratulations, which manages to both unnerve and humble. Friendliness flows as freely as the beer and elderflower alternatives. He puts down the tea and gulps hard on a half pint as they generously and optimistically wet the baby's head. Seven and a half months too early or twenty-two hours too late, depending. The beer sits thickly at the top of his gullet for a few uncomfortable moments before being granted safe passage, a hidden focal point for his uneasiness. He had prepared himself to lie to Liz and Sam, not the whole village.

'To baby Joshi,' toasts the pub landlord.

'Baby Joshi!'

Knowing he will not be able to stop himself from crying out if another such toast is made, he downs the remains of his half in spite of his trouble swallowing and quickly takes another. He is ready to drown his insides if that is the only way to trick his body into a different response.

Better to deflect all round. Swerve the baby talk so that he cannot be accused of being fraudulent at a later date, when they find out. He is willing to talk about anything. With the men the discussion is cricket and cricket only, exchanging views on the failure of the English team to capitalize on the promise they'd shown less than three hours ago.

'Bloody bunch of premature ejaculators,' spits one, with a brio that feels out of place in bucolic Sussex and more in tune with the rum-fuelled disenchantment of a Leicestershire living room filled with the cigarette smoke of Puppa and his friends.

'They can't keep it up for more than a couple of hours. Bunch of lard arses. All preening and no action.'

To the women he talks about the county recycling scheme, school waiting lists, and the easiness of making an Indian savoury spice cake. No one wants to speak about the asylum centre. He feels embarrassed to even bring it up. Disloyal and embarrassed.

Liz is forthright on all topics including a rundown on a tried-and-tested spice cake recipe using courgette, carrot and frozen peas. Like Claud she too has thrown herself into the new world, knowing that if she could not understand everything about religion – too many gods, a cast of thousands – she could at least understand the food. No, not understand the food, but master it.

'Bloody woman,' complained Puppa down the phone after one wet bank holiday get together. 'We drove all this way expecting a nice rib of beef and Yorkshire pud, and she serves us this tasteless, watery thali in cereal bowls! We had to stop at the services on the way home to make up for it.'

He heard Ma shouting exasperatedly in the background, from her tone probably not the first time that day. Any longer than an hour in the car and they were usually set to kill each other.

'The woman's trying, Ganno, eh? I don't see you making suet pastry for your kidney and steak pud when Claud and the boy visit.'

'I expect people to take me as they find me. And so should they. That way neither of us would have to endure another bland lunch whilst making stupid comments on the weather to calm their bloody nerves. Yes, I know it is windy today. Any fool can see that. My car was being shunted on the motorway by strong side winds but that doesn't make me want to deliver a five-minute speech on it. Know why? Because the weather is bloody boring! These people you have married into are so scared of putting a foot wrong they can't think of anything else to say. Speak your mind, man! Tell us your fears about what's happening to pension funds, the wear and tear on your 4x4, your worry of what brown-skinned sweat might do to your John Lewis cushions, or the future of your lovely farmhouse filled with brown babies, whose shitty arses you'll be required to wipe on occasion. Tell us about your fingers covered in Paki shit and the road that led you to it. But most importantly, give me bread and beef dripping and be done with it. No more of these chicken tikka skewers that come from a packet and pong of dishrag. Ha! Give me some bloody taste!'

When Liz hands him a piece of cake from the WI stall, smelling damp and moist with stored apples, he does not look at her hands lest his eyes give him away. Liz is nothing like Sam, but she too must have her worries.

'I sweat all night over this baby,' he begins, hoping he can be her mouthpiece, a ventriloquist's dummy for her fears. 'If I'm like this now, how will I cope when he's actually here?'

If the collection of cells has to be personified, it can only be a He. Has to be He. Amal does not have faith in Claud's genetic code and its ability to battle the might of tenacious, studious, subcontinental DNA. Ma was unable to fight Puppa's short and tubby string of cells. What chance, freckle-skinned, copper-haired Claud?

'Oh, no! You mustn't! This is the part you should be enjoying. Plenty enough time to worry, son of mine. Plenty of things to be worrying about. Safest time of a baby's life is when they're cosy in Mum's tum. Where they have no argument with the world.'

'And afterwards?'

'It's hard to live up to that same level of protection. Nothing compares. I suppose that's why they spend so many years hating you for it. Becoming little shits.'

'Is that how your felt when you were carrying Claud? Like her ultimate protector?'

'Actually I was in shock for most of it. We'd only been married three months, and I'd just started a new job sub-editing at the *Argus*. I think I spent the first twenty weeks pretending that it wasn't happening. You're much more looked after these days. Clinics and health visitors and everything. Back then, they didn't give a stuff. As long as you could shove a bottle into its mouth and didn't kill it, they left you alone.'

'It's true,' says a woman from the WI stand who has come to both retrieve her plate and butt in. As her eyes convey, she is alert to the thieving potential of the dark visitor, Liz or no Liz. 'The midwife left me alone in the labour room for an hour so she could go and have a sandwich with the ward sister. Corned beef and salad cream, with some jelly off the dinner trolley for afters. I'll never forget it.'

Maternity anecdotes make him feel ever more the foreign newcomer. Genteel china-clinked laughter. Liz doubles up more exuberantly than the others as if to hastily close what should never be opened up before a son-in-law, leaving him enlightened but bemused. When they have finished, the woman is quick to snatch back the plate.

'You should talk to your wife about these things. Make sure you're looking after her,' Liz says gently, giving him the good sense that a stupid boy needs. 'Samuel was very good with me when I was going through that. I think that's why they invented marriage: so you can make someone sweat in the middle of the night besides yourself.'

He always thought it was only Sam who made bad jokes to detract from his discomfort. He is wrong. There has never been any antagonism towards Liz, she is too benign for that, but something in what she says, a generosity, warms him towards her in a way he has never considered before. That she can be confided in like a friend. He suddenly feels protective towards her, ready to stand up to Sam the next time she is bullied or shown the slightest impatience; as if this can make up for over three years of indifference and complicity in Puppa's scathing opinion of her.

'Quiet as a mouse Englishwoman who enjoys playing the little wife.'

Puppa is a bastard in his judgements, and no matter how hard he tried to shake it, the description stuck. Sticks.

Claud should be treated the same way, like a friend who is ready to hear anything, any confession of failings. Is that not the point of husbands and wives? Once you learn to keep things to yourself it becomes a bigger well. Ample enough to hold your secrets. His has become a bottomless pit where worry floats with fear, floats with resentment, floats with dissatisfaction, floats with indecision. Did he do right by either of them, in marrying her? Had he thought hard enough about how their future would be, not the house and the car, but their day-to-day future; whether they could stand to be in the same car together, how they would divvy up the chores, and the outcome of any arguments at the supermarket checkout. All the stuff that is not covered in the non-stop fuck-fest pre-marriage, where cocktails are never bitter, and nothing is dirtied by domesticity. Nothing that can be muted by the detailed lists, footnotes and card indexes of serious wedding day preparation, either.

His has been a three-year period of preparation, of making mistakes and learning to correct them. Of forgetting those lessons and messing up again, before seeking new ways to avoid discord, such as the most recent one: staying out of the house; leaving work and spending half the night listening to music in the car because it made things easier than talking back to hormonal barb wire.

During his introductory lessons to Christianity, the

young reverend coaching him (earnestly and in detail, as if he were counting down to a school exam) remarked with some envy on the freshness of one's early marriage years when everything about each other was still not known. That he would find beautiful mystery in the mundane everyday situations that drove the world. It was a sensible notion that should have stuck with him more than any of the Church teachings if he had not been so caught up with discussing bloody frescos. Even as a child he had always liked a mystery. But there have been three years of mysteries on both their parts and he is tired of it. Tired from not enough sleep, and from this constant process of learning. When do the lessons end? When can they finally settle into their marriage and start to be happy?

There is something resolute in Liz's manner that gives him hope. Claud has Sam's bossiness but in every other way she is Liz's mirror, a time-tunnel to her sixth decade: the slight frame that has thickened with age without turning to fat; the jawline that continues to defy gravity by curving to a gentle point under the mouth; the hair, of a darker copper than her daughter, but still with the same thickness and lustre. He watches her as she playfully creeps up behind Sam and pinches his bum whilst he is in mid-spiel to a group of tourists who have put down their cameras and cakes to listen to a five-minute lecture on local concerns. Sam jumps at the suddenness of the move, at which everyone ham-fistedly stifles giggles, as if this is some regional theatre being acted out before them. But he remains as is, not turning round once until he has finished his point. There is no need. He recognizes the touch like a fingerprint. So close to him, it is virtually his own. Now their hands are locked, her nestling closer to him, his body slightly curving to accommodate her, and as if connected to the same battery, she too starts to speak on the perils of the proposed centre. Whether husband or wife, one must always be ready to welcome the other and speak with their voice. That is his lesson for today. Amen.

Left to his own devices, he finds himself doing a Sam and wandering alone around the Green. Passing a bench one of the older WI woman calls him to sit down.

'Come and have a rest. Too many children here.'

'Yes. Noisy, isn't it? I won't stop, though. I'm walking-off my cake.'

'People should only have one each, like they do in China. They're exhausting the planet with these screaming monsters. Some shouldn't have any at all. It's overrated, parenthood.'

He makes several laps as if he is being sponsored for his efforts. At every turn making sure he now avoids the old woman, whose words rattle him, he is drawn to the presence of the pole, no less phallic and authoritative than earlier. If there is any dormant belief left inside he should feel the gifts of pagan fertility bestowed upon him; some tiny seed to convince him that it is worth trying again.

That what they have suffered is a minor hiccup in the history of their future family. His ears close to the sound of bells being jangled from a nearby table, rattling and ringing, an amateur medley to mark the Herald of Spring, where every farm animal and villager is primed and aching to reproduce. Just not them.

He takes refuge in the church. The crowd has begun to leave their activities at the fringes of the Green and converge towards its centre. From the corner of his eye he expects to see the tug-of-war rope being coiled out, and suitable men conscripted into one side or other. Teeth-clenching rivalries between country houses and workmen's cottages have long since lost their validity in the wake of the mass exodus of the late '60s and '70s. Now they are lucky to muster an army fit enough for a game that pits country versus visiting townies or, if the ranks have swelled, the village versus the rest of Sussex.

We are scared of no man! Normans, Saracens, County Councils! We will take all comers!

He hurries past the Green and down the path that leads to the cemetery gates before he is spotted and volunteered. He has taken the bearings of the in-laws, both distracted with other matters; Sam now holding court at the pub steps; Liz helping with the litter patrol. Already his excuse is mapped out should he be found and questioned: he was taking a long shit in the pub on account of the berry flan.

The church, originally Norman, with Saxon, Victorian, Edwardian and Silver and Golden Jubilee additions, stands at the bottom of the lane overlooking the cemetery, and beyond that, the Green and the pub. The path is a cut-through from one side of the village to the other, one that avoids the worst of the hill; the building itself is a local point of pride, with well-tended gardens and a row of highly polished slatted benches, but otherwise it is ignored bar Sunday ritual. Loved, but hurriedly attended to, like a long-standing pet slowly on its way out.

On previous visits, smug with newfound knowledge, he would take a detour whilst Claud and her parents meandered over misshapen vegetables at the organic market. His head rang as high and clear as that marvellous iron construction in the bell tower, devouring ornamental woodwork; dark, circular hymn tables and coved placards honouring mothers' unions. Relishing the cool air of the chancel; feeling the smoothness of the stonework, and tracing his fingers over the deep-set engraving that adorned it.

The Tudors were ahead of the village's origins by a few hundred years, but everything here is in praise of the rose and more meadow flowers, as if, drunk on the beauty of the Downs, the stonemasons felt an obligation to incorporate the bucolic landscape within worship.

From a succession of furtive visits – a thirty-minute detour when work meetings were booked anywhere off the M25 – he has come to the conclusion that villages most often got the churches that they deserved. Half the reason he converted was not to pray within the sometimes handsome, but often utilitarian red-brick boxes of the modern towns. He appreciated a beautifully embroidered kneeler, but did not approve of an array of soft furnishings scattered across pews, or worse, rows of richly upholstered chairs in red or hunting-green gauze that smelt depressingly similar to the municipal furniture of conference centres or service stations. The no-nonsense stained-glass, thrifty in spirit and lacking in decoration, suited those streets lined with post-war semis and their Tudor gables and tightly paved driveways.

He can never admit to Ma and Puppa that it is architectural snobbery that has convinced him of a specific Christ, hardily worshipped from such taken-for-granted splendour as here. If Claud's family had come from Milton Keynes he would have put up more of a fight, found a way to argue out of converting; treating the cultural clash like a structured debate with reasons for and against. There would be no emotional element, no epiphany or pull from his guts to illustrate his mindset; just blatantly taking advantage of those who disagreed with each other on how strength of belief should be measured.

Often he comes here, bored, angry, though those feelings never linger for long; not when there is so much to look at. Put him anywhere holy and he has the eyes of a newborn, constantly registering and filtering the surroundings.

It was the very serious curate leading his conversion who was to blame, developing his studied appreciation for something that had previously been passed off as a curiosity. A cursory forty minutes was spent at each class checking that he had done his homework. The remainder of the ninety minutes was taken with a series of antique art books with enlarged colour plates.

Christopher's subject of interest was Russian icons. Probably the closest he would get to camp, he thought, during their discussions on religious art. English and Italian Formalists versus ostentatious works composed almost entirely in gilt. Now, as is usual, his attention is first taken with the imposing painted cross suspended at the head of the altar, a surprisingly Catholic touch for so English a village. A Norman souvenir, it stands five foot by three; a pleasingly severe depiction of sufferance and benediction. Austerity aside, as perhaps a reflection of their being in the country, lush and lazily bountiful, he looks for the slightest smirk across Christ's tight lips.

None of you have it hard the way I do.

Many times he has sat in the twelfth pew – further enough away from the door to deflect conversation with flower-changing busybodies, and the nearest he can get to fully appreciate the crucifix in all its severe, glossy detail without craning his neck. Sat open-mouthed, like stone, willing the one who died for our sins to absorb his petty frustrations: a sore cock and balls from Claud's shagging schedule; wanting to spend his weekends anywhere else other than a village tucked into the hills.

There were certain pictures of Shiva, Ganesh, and Lord Krishna that had the same effect up in Leicester, but he had never shared this with his parents. There, worship was domestic, visiting temples something that was done while in India or during the bigger festivals. His experience of home worship was all backroom incense, and pins and needles from sitting an hour cross-legged.

Ma and Puppa would often equate the rolled eyes and the sulking at having to put aside the bike, computer game, long-planned dalliance with a girl to his godlessness. It was not the act he was fighting, more a sense of suffocation; his inability to take prayer seriously, when just yards away from the front step he had stubbed out an illicit cigarette the night before, having to creep down at 6 a.m. to scrub it clean for fear of detection. His attention was most often taken with what was directly above his head, his bedroom, which offered a more alluring and pleasurable array of distractions. (His temple was under the duvet. It was the same for all the lads in his class.)

Up until he married his experience of life was cramped. Home: small rooms; university halls: small rooms; rented studio: small room; first one-bedroom flat: small, low rooms. The spatial dimensions of the church are what hook him. The fact that he can sink into the pew and feel insignificant and no longer aware of himself; so taken is he by sensations of fascination and fear. The city temple north of Birmingham gives a similar feeling, but what puts the church forward is the fact that he is often the only person there. Ten minutes alone in there and it becomes his own place; God's House on a temporary let.

But there are things to put a cap on his sentimentality, namely the understanding that staring at the face of Christ is unable to take him back in time to prevent what was lost. That the Crucifixion is no adequate shoulder for the ache that fills him, the size of a boulder settled in the place where a baby should be. He does not feel the oncoming lightness often attributed to a pensive posture facing the altar; nor can he understand how those who find themselves in unexpected, dire circumstances, can leave this building after a few minutes, an hour, and claim to be healed.

The stillness is a comfort. Perhaps it is the coolness of the interior, and the silence, that pushes him into a state where comfort is felt: a starting point for prayer. There is stillness in the house in Richmond too, but here the rooms are overwhelmingly personal, shell-firing memories at every turn to the point where only methodically sweeping the front drive or hosing the bins can block them.

Except, there isn't complete silence. The louvres have been pulled open, allowing the pulse of the Herald to intrude with every heartbeat. Distracted now, he turns his head to catch it. Too close to be dismissed as white noise, his overactive brain is no longer capable of filtering it out. Voices ringing, high and in unison; soaring sharply over claps and cheers.

It is not the tug of war that has brought them together, he realizes, but the school choir. They are singing the song '*You're beautiful*' to an accompaniment from a couple of guitars and a flute. Another strange display of village insularity and narcissism, he thinks, until the penny drops, and he remembers how most of them were dressed in daffodil yellow and crocus white.

The voices are young, nervous, and wilfully attention-seeking. They bring the reality of the Herald, and a vision of what Sam wishes for his grandchild. He can see his kid, four, five years from now, standing plaited and clad in Barbour in a country field somewhere, singing the same kind of songs. He sees, even before his baby has breathed his first, this scheming for ownership; how they will take his child away from him.

Ma and Puppa have the same plans, though their tongues are loose to the point of stream of consciousness. Too excited to hold anything back, they have no secrets; itself an admission that they have waited too long for this moment, their first grandchild made real.

'We've told Auntie Ginny to get permission to extend the house at the back, so we can all come over next year after rainy season. It will be warm but not uncomfortable. Perfect for a toddler.'

There is more than just hopefulness in their voices. Under the pragmatism lies excitement, and middle-aged mischief that comes from asking Puppa's lazy sister to get her arse in gear and fix the Kolkata house up. The urgency is there too, of course. The urgency never leaves them. Baby's foot must touch his blood soil whilst he is still in an underdeveloped, inarticulate state. The mish-mash of his origins can be taken for granted, so long as everyone starts off on an equal footing.

In-laws on all sides are ready to lay down their food-grabbing arms if they can all get a little of what they want in those first twelve months. After that, it is for the parents themselves to decide.

Ordinarily he is hardened to children's singing. He finds choirs twee and emotionally manipulative. At the first sign of them in shopping centres or rugby matches he heads the other way, self-satisfied with his verisimilitude. He despises the way cuteness is deployed to cream cash from innocent shoppers. Donations of ten pounds to vaguely explained charities is mugging at its worst. Kids brainwashed into doing good works, even at a young age, dazzled by the lure of garish costumes and guaranteed attention.

They have not talked of specifically how they will raise their child. Still overtaken with relief, the unspoken understanding is that common sense will dominate over interfering parents and exacting manuals. There has already been too much of both.

Theirs would not be paraded about like Sussex show ponies. There were plenty of cool, funky children they could take as their template. Ones that were fully engaged with other children without dance competitions and singing around bonfires. Claude had exactly that kind of upbringing throughout her primary years. That was how he knew she wanted the complete opposite.

But the children in the choir have been coached well. For all the wonder of the song, they play upon its sense of melancholy, conjuring shades of grey they have no right to know about. Choral coercion. A sadness snaking under the church door, coiling around his arm and twisting it behind his back. Twisting to the point of tears. More tears.

He has not come to church to cry. The wetness sitting on his cheekbones becomes as familiar as the stillness that envelopes him. It floats around him in thick bubbles, like humidity; something that cannot just be physically felt, but grabbed, captured.

Bastard children. Even at this distance they have the

power to paralyse him. His legs are glued in their cross position, as frozen as Claud's impenetrable eggs.

～～～

His phone buzzing in his pocket sends his left leg into spasm. Hari.

'Your family is seriously screwed up, man.'

'Watch your language. I'm sitting in a church.'

'Bad choice of words. Unlucky, is what I meant. A real case of bad timing.'

Now that he is over the shock, and embedded deep in their duplicity, Hari has reverted to his trusted self: dramatist, stirrer.

'Your call is the thing that's bad timing, son. I really have to go.'

In spite of the rabble-rousing tone, something in Hari's voice centres him; perhaps the same element that comes from the altar cross, whatever that unspeakable element may be. He is hooked on stillness, an addict, clinging on to those that can anchor him.

Maybe this is the point of prayer. Like an entry point. An invisible door located deep in this silence. You just have to keep your mouth shut and your thoughts together long enough to work out where it is. If this is the case, I have become a believer, he thinks, shying away from nothing. I believe in the power of prayer . . . so long as it can get me what I want: patience, a time-machine, a stronger cellular structure, the ability not to apportion blame.

'You're right. I agree with you absolutely,' he says, aware that Hari's voice has risen in volume and pitch, and hoping this cover-all masks his wandering. Hari's only venture inside a church was down to his best man duties. He once boasted of taking a piss outside the convent on Westbourne Grove during his student days as 'a laugh'.

'You're sounding very distant, 'Mal. Otherworldly. Have they made you saint in there? Has Jesus performed his magic?'

'Don't take the piss, Hari.'

'Ha! That's mature. So it's all right for you to swear, is it?'

'Acceptable in the circumstances. I'm defending the faith.'

'You only like it down there because it's pretty. You wouldn't be so fast to wave a tambourine down some community centre in Peckham if that was the only option. You can't fool me the way you do them.'

'And even that I do badly.'

'Ha! That's my boy!'

'What are you even doing calling me? They say a respectful distance in these situations is always best.'

'Like a priest to his flock.'

Hari can proclaim heresy to his heart's content, so long

as it keeps him on the phone. Nonsense acting as sound barrier between him and the kids choir; him and the continual rolling in his chest; the weak, hollow feeling in his teeth and the new, sudden itchiness of his skin, that makes him want to shed his outer form and start again, light and unburdened. But more than that, it is the skin-tone that binds them. Family. He would never speak this way to anyone else.

'That's always been your problem, 'Mal,' – the lazy drawl in Hari's voice makes Amal wonder where he is, sofa, pub, bed – 'I've never been very good with boundaries. You're in church because?'

'I'm hiding from the glorified village fete. Long story.'

'They haven't taken it well, then?'

'They don't know. Not yet. Claud has to decide when, not me.'

'Yes, best leave it to her. It's a man's job, after all.'

He takes it, the barbs, same as he takes his wife's. Day-to-day abuse delivered down phone lines. Daily, like cornflakes; as fulfilling as prayer. It is a masochism that always put him on the lower rung in previous relationships – lippy girls who told him he never did anything right, until he got out his credit card – a facet of character best suited to temporary residence here, where both the start and end point is one of sin.

'If I didn't have guts I wouldn't have driven down here,' he says flatly, as unconvinced as his listener.

'I know you do,' Hari says suddenly, welling with an unfamiliar remorse. 'I've no idea how I'd react in the circumstances. Nowhere near as sound as you're doing, I imagine.'

'Don't know about that. I'm . . . muddling along. Passing time until the day's over.'

'I shouldn't have called you, I'm sorry. I'm sitting in the pub, bored because the person I'm meeting is twenty minutes late. It's pathetic. Allow me to take leave and go fuck myself.'

'Not before you tell me your news. You haven't called for no reason.'

'It's nothing . . .' He hesitates, embarrassed. 'Just bored. Other people have the sense not to answer when they see my name. Not you.'

'Sure?' He is still in the market for distraction. If religious icons and a restored nave cannot do the job, maybe the mantle should be taken by the selfish, the trivial.

'Yup. No different to usual. Empty mind and all that.'

He feels hollow once Hari has hung up ('Look after yourself, man. Look after her'), ill at ease with the uncertainty in his friend's voice. Hari's desire to self-censor is unheard of in other situations – shagging at funerals, nicking the odd present at wedding receptions – prompting him to wonder at which elements of their ordeal have driven this response. Notes of wistfulness maybe; that this tragedy is not his to experience first hand. Or is that just how he, Amal, now thinks of it? Willing himself to swap places with Hari and become the outsider.

Then, a second phone interruption before he even has a chance to take his hand out of his pocket. Others are at fault for his inattention to prayer. He would be faithful, devout, if it were not for these distractions.

The polysynthetic ring tone he chose as jokingly retro, pleasingly base next to Claud's bog-standard Blackberry audio signature, sounds just as tinny and cheap as it did moments earlier. No, worse than before, shamefully so, as its cartoonish top notes bounce from icon to font to altar steps. Even the echo seems to slide despairingly off each hard surface, slick of unwanted matter; like a Teflon pan coming into contact with mono-saturated fats.

Similarly, his arse cannot help but skid across the pew, as he struggles to fish the phone from his pocket. It is as if the actual building knows he is an outsider, and refuses his attempt to take root. It renders the shelter into something temporary and of a flimsier construction than the one in his mind; pavilion bench or suburban bus stop.

Try as he might, he will never fit into this town. Even in places where he hides away. No matter how well-worn his wellington boots are or how stained his Barbour Mac, the countryside will always reject him.

'How are you feeling?' he asks, softly, hearing her

breath, and immediately wishing it was not this phone, but her nestled against his ear, her weight pushing into his neck, perfume filling his nose and mouth.

'Better,' says the voice on the other end. Claud's, thick with warmth and hoarse with crying.

A whisper that brings something back from their wedding, small utterances that only the other could hear: I'm bricking it; You're beautiful; the ring won't fit.

'I've slept. Washed my face.'

'That's good. We're leaving the Herald now.'

'I think I've had enough of being on my own.'

'I'm really pleased you called, Claud. It makes me happy.'

He realizes his prayer as he says it. Silence paving the way for honesty. Anger and guilt, banished.

He hears her intake of breath before replying; a pause where an unspoken apology is accepted.

'Come home, 'Mal. I'm missing you.'

The house smells of baking which alarms all of them. Like her mother everything she touches becomes burnt and inedible. From the front door they get a clear view of her, standing by the sink drying Liz's mixing bowl and wooden spoon with a look of deep concentration, seeming not to notice that they are back. She does not rouse until Sam has one foot in the kitchen. She is wearing one of Liz's old evening dresses, high-fronted and backed. The blue satin gives an incredibly high gloss, so much so that under the kitchen halogens he is sure that he can make out his reflection staring back at him, open-mouthed, incredulous. Everything about the silhouette clashes with the soberness of her chores — the movie star on her day off. With her face scrubbed of make-up, her hair pulled back into a loose ponytail she looks younger and more vulnerable, as spirited and helpless as a gangly teenager.

'I thought you wouldn't be back until much later. I wanted to surprise you with something.'

Liz and Sam splutter over one another, something along the lines of, 'you shouldn't have gone to so much trouble', but now that they are reassured that nothing has been set on fire, they are nonplussed. Liz has won a seventh prize in the tombola. A smallish object held in a wooden case the size of a small book which she will not reveal until dinner.

'Time and place for everything, you impatient people. Curiosity killed the cat or whatever that cliché was. This is the first time I've won anything. Isn't it unbelievable?'

'It would be, if you hadn't given them a painting worth a hundred quid,' grumbles Sam, who has talked of nothing else since he heard how much it cost from an eagle-eye shopper on the Green. He was only persuaded not to take it back after he was assured by his son-in-law that he had lost the receipt.

Amal is staring at Claud's stomach, whose overwhelming flatness is emphasized by the narrowness of the dress's cut and the clinginess of the fabric. Realizing where he is looking, she hurriedly covers herself in the butcher's stripe apron hanging in the peg by the back door, both of them hoping that the rush of motion proves distracting to overattentive parents who tend to pick up everything. The look she fires back is one of deep hurt, shocked that he would blatantly focus on that particular part of her.

'Let me help you with that, darling. You were never any good with tying ribbons. You had a good nap?'

'Been up for ages, Mum. Still got morning sickness. Threw up over my jumper.'

'That's quite all right, darling. You can wear whatever you like.'

She smoothes Claud's hair lovingly, strokes her indulgently. In the space of three steps both of them have regressed to the period when Liz originally wore the dress, a wedding reception in the late seventies when Claud was no older than five. Amal realizes then how the dress is familiar to him, from one of the family pictures in the living room.

'I was going to come and join you, only I couldn't find Amal's keys, and the walk is . . .'

'Inadvisable for a woman in your condition,' affirmed Sam. 'It was slippery on the path today. You did the right thing by staying here.'

A look passes between Liz and Sam to express the horror of what could happen. There but for the grace of God; their one true time to put faith in Jesus. It bounces between them before being tossed in Amal's direction like he is part of some football keepy-uppy group trick. Rural life has hardened them to the namby-pamby nature of suburban protectiveness. Health and safety Nazis can go and take a running jump in their eyes; Pasteurization is pooh-poohed, fruit and vegetables continue to be bought in pounds and ounces, but when it comes to their daughter, their only child, cotton wool is not simply needed, it is mandatory. Life-giving oxygen made solid.

If this is how they act when she is healthy, he wonders what will happen if he blurts it out by mistake, or if one look too many, one apron cover-up is correctly interpreted. She would be put on immediate bed rest with a twenty-four-hour nurse posted outside the door. He knows there will be an interrogation, and that it will be long and unpleasant. Liz will neglect to call him 'my son' until matters are satisfactorily concluded. Sam will do what he wished he did that first afternoon he was brought down to Sussex, and bare his fangs.

Claud shares none of the dread that comes with his fortune-telling. She is treating her lie in the same way she does her career: single-minded, 100 per cent committed. The baking is the biggest indicator of that. She wants, needs everything to be perfect.

Liz and Sam go upstairs to change, leaving them standing at the oven, watching uncertainly for signs of flour-egg-sugar alchemy. Her earlier warmth on the phone now burning with the cakes. Funny how he now feels more comfortable with them than with her. The power of paganism makes friendships of men.

'What is it?'

'Carrot cake. There was a bunch in the fridge looking like they were about to turn.'

'Waste not want not.'

'Precisely. We should practise some of that at home. We buy far too much food, 'Mal. No one's ever around to eat it.'

Meaning he is not around to eat it or cook it. For at least a third of the twenty-one days, when he sat in his car and talked himself out of his fear, she has been left on her own, steaming fish and ready prepped vegetables in the plug-in machine that promises miracles for hopeless cooks.

'So what's in the cake, Claud?'

'Carrots. I told you.'

'I know that. I meant, what else you put in it. Which recipe you used.'

'Flour . . . and other stuff, all right? I thought I was doing something useful, 'Mal. Didn't expect to be questioned on every element that's gone in it.'

'I'm just interested. Not trying to start an argument. I just can't remember you ever baking before.'

'Oh, I have, plenty of times.'

She had been so open with him about the baby. Every sensation that flooded through her in those three weeks was shared, making him feel the shift in hormones to the point where he was certain that change was happening in his body too. Simpatico. They had laughed about it. Now she wants him to know nothing about her. Recipes are secret, the workings of her body, private. He is eligible for the firing squad just for looking at her. When the darkness in her eyes pauses its intolerant transmission they exude mystery – more mystery – and a desire not to be read. She expects him to be as blank as her. Two canvases, like the junk they bought in Battle; stony-faced, without an opinion between them. At the oven or elsewhere she has no use for him. Even the need for his manky sperm is negligible.

'Let me do something. Chuck me over that dishcloth.'

She stays where she is at the draining board.

'It's fine. I got it covered.'

He tells her about the maypole, hoping there is something in the history and comedy of the Green that will thaw her, but her joints remain frozen and ungiving. If they hung ribbon from her she could be danced around, worshipped. No one would be any the wiser.

If she has guessed his true fear of the pole, that he had Ophelia-type visions of her wailing to the fertility gods in an Anglo Saxon paean to the Bollywood melodrama, disrupting everyone's afternoon, she does not show it.

How to communicate that fear and break the ice? He remembers reading an online report, probably bogus, which mentioned that six per cent of victims of serious road traffic accidents – the ones who walked away miraculously with a scratch – stopped speaking for up to sixteen weeks after the incident. Her lips are folded thickly one under the other; thick folds like her curdled cake mixture.

For the second time today he thinks about channelling Puppa and using a physical act to shock her into her senses. A shake or slap. Something he would not dare try here. His anger must find a more effective channel before he does something regrettable and dangerous in Sam's house.

He cools down outdoors. The garden is magnificent in its maturity and stamps on suburban aspirations, where single trees and timid bushes of hydrangea, rose and ivy are worshipped. His in-laws have had over thirty years to harness the rich orchard soil that backs the house, to preserve the wide tunnel of hard fruit trees planted in the last century, whilst allowing the invasion of newer, more alien greenery to flourish. Three decades in, there is no questioning the logic of the Japanese autumn ferns that form a lofty second wall along the existing brickwork, nor the kiwi fruit bushes planted in favoured west-facing soil, and whose branches lean widely in all directions until they almost touch their cousins of pear, apple and plum. Mistakes have been corrected along the way; the best places for patio slabs, walkways, bird baths and fish ponds have been tried and tried again until they were wholly satisfied that the right balance was reached – wild, well-tended, and in some parts, hidden and magical.

It makes Amal ashamed of their froufrou shrubbery in Richmond where each plant has been austerely potted and made separate from the others. The tightly packed Boxwood shrubs, cosmetically pleasing and well-mannered in their growth, and the pink Cordyline, whose spiky leaves shoot upwards from the earth, injecting a little rock 'n' roll into their young fogeyness whilst still continuing to complement the garden furniture. There is no contact from one plant to the next; even the roots, he suspects, mind their own business, each existing in its own alkaline-leaning bubble.

What does he know about nature? He has lived in five different houses through childhood, where gardens were for playing in, not maturing.

Sam is also outside, doing something out of view behind the arch of Sweet William, beyond which lies the swing seat where Claud swotted for her A-levels, and the sundial where she daydreamed about boys, and occasionally smoked with them. It is a job that requires changing into a pair of wellington boots and an old gardening jumper, a blue and cream Fair Isle, knackered at the elbows and much loved by moths everywhere else.

'Come and have a look at this, or not, if you can't make it,' he calls, louder than is necessary, and looking pointedly at Amal's shoes, as if to imply the distance involved from patio to muddy lawn has more significance than a mere stroll of a hundred or so yards. His son-in-law is labelled a city boy who does not like to get his hands dirty and will always be so. Nothing since the wedding has given him cause to change his mind. He pays no mind that Amal's brogues are already covered in dirt from the hike to the village and the trampled-in mud of the Green. A few more steps are not going to hurt.

He finds Sam standing over a freshly covered hole at the base of the sundial the size of a shoebox.

'We've had trespassers. Probably trying to steal the thing while we were at the Herald.'

'A fox?'

'Kids. A few gardens have been vandalized around here recently. Greenhouses smashed, urinating in rainwater barrels and the like. Didn't think they were the digging type though.'

'I thought it was animals that went round digging holes.'

'Our four-legged friends aren't that tidy, mate. Not in this country, anyway.'

They are standing among loose clumps of mud, which have sprayed across this part of the lawn, stubbornly sticking to the grass like the after effects of a howling storm. The covering of the hole, slightly domed and patted down, is neat and considered. Too neat for both animals and bored teenagers.

'Jesus Christ, look at the size of it! That's good turf they've mashed up.'

'That's a little harsh, isn't it? For the old blasphemy?'

'Say what I like in my own house! Don't believe in any of that crap, anyway. It's only your lot who follow that mumbo jumbo to the letter these days.'

'And who's "my lot" when they're at home?'

'Converts.'

This family will never forget what he has done. Never thank him enough.

Sam goes to check the shed rather than seeing what is underneath. He has over five hundred pounds worth of grass cutters and power tools piled one on top of another, of which only the lawn mower is regularly used. They are at the age where handymen are called in to take care of the rest. His father-in-law is active, but does not have enough faith in the strength of his joints to be going up and down ladders like a banana boy.

'Check the spade!'

'What?'

'If the kids have broken in, Sam, they'll have used the spade.'

'They might have brought their own. I told you, son, they're professionals.'

Son-in-law's lot, to be wrong at every turn.

His fingers burrow deep into the freshly dug earth. Though it is damp and matted to the touch, he is surprised how much it feels like something more familiar under his hands: dough mix. Surprised too at the profound thump that has returned in his chest. Every time he thinks it has gone, the raised pulse returns. Unless, of course, it is simply a matter of perception; that his heart has been beating at something close to sprint rate from the moment Claud came down the stairs yesterday afternoon and said disbelievingly that she thought something was wrong. Maybe it has never deflected since then. His body responses remaining on an emergency mode.

He is past wrist deep, half his forearm stained with dirt, before dough hits rocky road, a hard square object. He scrabbles to retrieve the box, aware of how dog-like his movements have become; quick and sharp, never allowing speed to deflect from accuracy. He feels the soil flying into his lap and, as he works, heat dappling his temples and forehead, every sensation pleasurable and exciting. The mindlessness of the animal, a dog with no cares aside from reuniting with his bone. A plastic box he can sink his teeth into, and grapple with. A human chew toy designed to take his mind off everything else.

The box is one of Liz's makeshift Tupperwares, an old

Chinese takeaway container stained pink and orange with age. Sandwiches or salad have been thrown out for a brown letter envelope sealed with tape. He is unsure whether this is for dramatic effect or for added protection, should the plastic fail to stay airtight for whatever reason. Neither is a good enough excuse. He rips it in a dense, echoing heartbeat, already knowing the identity of the digger — a thirty-something woman masquerading as Sussex hoodies — but still unsure as to what he will find.

It is a photo of him and Claud taken last weekend at Liz and Sam's. They are in their good clothes because of a Village Association dinner that the in-laws are holding. Look like a couple of Allsorts. He is wearing the pink grapefruit cashmere v-neck she gave him for Christmas; she is in a turquoise wrap dress bought that day because she wanted to start preparing her wardrobe for roomier gear.

The afternoon drive down had been a blast. She sang along to Blur, songs from their student days, poking fun whenever he joined in and got the words wrong. Couple of hours of harmless baiting, toasty from the fan heater, and enjoying each other's company. One of those days when everything is right about their choices and where they have ended up.

When Liz takes the shot on her digital, a Mother's Day present from both of them, the sheen threatens to fade altogether. The guests have just been laughing over a joke

Sam had made. Something along the lines of how many Poles does it take to change a light-bulb. The seats of Village Association pants moisten with this repertoire. Much of the same stuff has been bandied about all evening, all satisfied in the knowledge that it will never be them forced into this line of work; that no downturn will put them in the position of being seen as the lesser man. Catastrophe doesn't happen to hard-working, rambunctious taxpayers like themselves.

If there is tiredness in his face as he listens for the dreaded punch line, something that is guaranteed to be crass and wilful in its humiliation, he does not show it; smiling for the camera like a pro, always ready to leave nothing less than his best impression. It is the immigrant's millstone: even in the face of this smug, politically incorrect tediousness he will remain all eyes and teeth, determined never to be less than his most exemplary self. He ignores all the good sense that tells him his household is no different, where Puppa will curse all other native tongues and religions other than his own; only that Sussex is an indirect and far crueller beast. Sam can be throttled later on. Claud can be argued with upstairs. Liz's better glasses can be smashed against patio stones in exasperation for not bringing this rubbish to a halt.

Claud too can leave her irritation with him for another time. Her hand on his thigh is well aware of the stiffening that ripples through him as Sam continues his end of the pier entertainment. Though neither are facing one another, he knows her well enough to understand her displeasure is twofold: that he could ruin the prospect of a good picture by indulging his frown lines or tightening his lip; and that, after all this time, he is still capable of getting annoyed with what is just some light joking to distract their guests from draining the drinks cupboard before time.

It is not so much that he has taken offence, more that he should learn not to become offended at all; that he should sit back and take it like the Kolkata bitch he is. Train himself to hide it better from her, at the very least.

Not even the clarity of a digital print can ease the tension in the photograph, as if they are living, breathing human photo-shoppers, consciously editing themselves when Liz fumbles with the capture button she is still unable to master. It is left to his wife to save him.

'Tracey Jacks! Left home without waning. Tracey Jacks! At five in the morning,' she whispers in his ear in her best Mockney accent. A throwback to their afternoon of Blur-induced merrymaking.

He laughs out loud, as Liz clicks, surprised and delighted as a child being sung his favourite nursery rhyme, not just because it is a tune that gives pleasure but because how well she knows him, responds to his need. He is lucky. He should admit it more.

In the photo, Claud shines as much as he does. They

have a baby inside them and everything about their future is radiant and full of good hopes. They have been groomed to be picture perfect; a walking advertisement that a marriage such as theirs can be free of discord and immune to outside interference. Hers is a thick hide, seasoned over a lifetime; his from a six-month crash course leading up to the wedding when he was told by everyone to iron out his flaws.

'You should only marry this girl if she makes you happy,' said Ma, 'we never brought you up to think that we would stand in your way. We're not like those maniacs in the news who chop the hands and heads off their children . . . but, you must not shame this family. Don't bring any bad behaviour into your marital home; anything that will cause her family to say, "hmm, I suppose that's how he was brought up. We shouldn't expect anything different." If I hear anything along those lines, receive any late-night phone calls from unimpressed mother-in-law, I'll come down there and beat your shitty arse.'

'What she means is, we wish you all the luck in the world, Amal, but you must watch your back. Her people look like a bunch of backstabbers. Never trust them for an instant.'

'Oh, why couldn't you have married a simpler girl, if you wanted English, sonny? It's not been six weeks since the wedding and already I feel the complications. Mark my words, it will get worse.'

Lodged under the photo is her hospital wristband. He takes his time touching it, gingerly, as if his fingertips will pop into open blisters the moment he makes contact. Everything about the heat, the drama of the hospital seems to have been condensed into this flimsy plastic loop with her identity starkly penned in biro: Brown-Joshi, C. How does fear come in a package so small? What made her want to bury it?

Then he remembers the collection of cells, and the power of something so minuscule, in that moment understanding everything that the wristband represents. He dry gags a couple of times before expelling a miserly trail of watery spit into his child's grave. It is not a malicious act. He just cannot think where else he can flob undetected.

'Nothing here,' Sam calls. 'They didn't touch the shed. Got a little distracted putting the workbench away. Threw everything in the other day when it started raining without dismantling it first. Very sloppy job.'

He pockets the wristband before Sam comes back, grimacing as he pushes it down into his pocket, knowing that this somehow buries the baby deeper than Claud's first efforts. Out of sight. Non-existent.

'You had any luck there? Look at you, up to your knees in mud, like a sand boy.'

'It's a Tupperware with a picture of me and Claud in it.'

'She's back doing the time capsules, is she? That takes me back.'

'It's normal, then?'

'It is in this house. She's never been the type of girl to keep scrapbooks or anything like that. You know that for yourself. I bet those wedding photos are still languishing in an envelope in a bottom drawer waiting for one of you to paste them into an album.'

'That's very true, sir.'

'Look around this garden, Amal. I guarantee there'll be two of three other Tupperwares within spitting distance. She was always doing them as a kid. Why do you think we don't have any proper Tupperwares left indoors? She used them all up! Sent Liz mental, until we realized that it was just her way of understanding things. Her favourite sandals got the same treatment once she'd grown out of them. There's a Duke of Edinburgh's Bronze Award lying around somewhere too, I think.'

Sam's forgetfulness of his earlier indignation shows a fragility of mind that softens his indignation at 'sand boy', making him feel protective for the third time that afternoon. Aware he is being led down a path of humanity towards his in-laws, everything about this visit has made it so, he pulls back, resisting the urge to complete the cycle with a reassuring pat on his father-in-law's shoulder.

'She likes souvenirs, that girl. Just doesn't like having them cluttered around.'

He thinks of their living room, piled with magazines but barren of mementos bar one enlarged wedding photograph taken on the church step.

Sam studies the picture with pursed lips, the skin cracked with too much beer. His heavy breathing suggests wonderment: how his little girl let herself get knocked-up by a guy who will only bring trouble. The birth of his first grandchild will only emphasize the alienness of its nuclear family; something that feels a little too modern for comfort in this sleepy village. The house was only connected to broadband last year. The latter half of this decade's social and technological advancement has yet to arrive.

'Good picture, mate. You look very smart, the pair of you.'

'Even with the food stain on my jumper?'

'We need to teach you how to be less messy with the lasagne. It was all over the tablecloth if I remember.'

'No, that was you and your red wine.'

'Ha! Touché! Very good. You shouldn't worry too much about it being ruined, mate. Liz would've made a copy. If I know her, probably three.'

He realizes now that the corners are already waterlogged from an unseen crack in the Tupperware and bleeding their colour. His fingers are stained with the red-black ink that dominates printer cartridges; wet with it, like soothing water mist from tropical rains, cooling all that is too hot to handle.

He feels the rush of blood through his ears as the implication reaches him. An understanding that makes him cold with fear at what he must do.

A quiet voice within him suggests he should say a little prayer because everything about the setting and of Claud's gesture is the closest he will get to a goodbye. Say a prayer and put your child to bed. Do not think of the toilet bowl about to be pulled from your Richmond bathroom and thrown into a plumber's skip. Pretend the garden is the place. Put your lips on Claud's face, and her stomach, and send your child off with a prayer.

All he can think of is the Serenity prayer taught to him by the patient conversion class priest. All this time he thought he had taken in nothing, and here were the words coming to him perfectly as he silently recites. He ignores the betrayal pangs that indicate an insult to his roots; that he chooses the prayer over something Hindi, a mantra, but he cannot grapple with that now. As a parent he can only put his child first.

But before he gets the chance to finish, he feels it snatched from his hands again. Sam is forcefully placing it back inside the Tupperware, without the envelope, before laying it in the hole. The only care he takes over the procedure is a final straightening of the box in its resting position, keeping up his job as the protector of Claud's flights of fancy.

'Stop daydreaming.'

'In a minute, Sam.'

'You can get all misty-eyed later, you sentimental so and so. I need a hand putting this soil back where we found it. Don't want our girl getting upset, do we?'

He gently throws a couple of mounds across the box, whilst Sam, impatient, and eager to get back indoors, kicks in his contribution. The covering with dirt is the completion of his prayer, the best he can hope for. He is prepared to lie through dinner if it means stealing more private time outdoors. Let them think he is smoking, growing aggressive tumours in his chest, because of an urgent nicotine fix. Let them think what they like.

'You're looking after her, aren't you, Amal? I was worried about how pale she was looking earlier until I remembered how sick Liz used to get in the early stages. You have to be attentive, mate. She'll be relying on you these next few months. We all are.'

'What do you see when you look at that picture?'

'I don't get you, son.'

'You were studying it. What did you see?'

'My daughter and son-in-law having a laugh in the living room. What is this?'

'And? What else?'

'Don't tell me you're into all this symbolism crap. Has Liz's rubbish rubbed off on you?'

'I'm not that easily led, Sam. Coming from an Indian family, remember.'

'Oh yes, your religion. Sorry, your old religion. Ha!'

His laugh is like a kick to the guts. Sam has always had him down as a perfect fool: malleable, docile, and loaded. He must have split his sides with the prospect of torturing him as he walked Claud down the aisle. His eyes narrow in this continual sizing-up, wondering how best to take him on.

'Oh, I get it. You want to start a fight. I don't see a half-caste baby if that's what you're trying to make me say. I wouldn't disrespect either you or my grandchild that way.'

'I see the future. Me and my wife looking forward to something life-changing. Frightening, but life-changing. Did you notice how we were grinning with the terror of it?'

'Like a Cheshire cat. Relax a little, Amal. What you're going through is the same as any other father-to-be.'

'I am relaxed . . . Which is what?'

'Shitting yourself! Ha! Every bloke feels that way with their first. You should talk about these things instead of winding yourself up.'

'Clear off, Sam. Leave me to get on with this. Look how much mess you're making.'

'Oi! You're the one badgering me on what I see. You can't get the hump 'cos you don't like the answer.'

'That's only one observation. I want more.'

'You're a financial analyst, not a forensic scientist. Who gives a stuff what I see?'

'I do. I'm family.'

'That can be rectified.'

'What's that supposed to mean?'

'I'm just teasing, son. Having a little fun with you! This is just another example of why you should lighten up. You're always so tense when you come here. I can see it in your face.'

He fought with Puppa several times in his teens. Puppa, high on rum and a bad night at the tables, sorely overestimating his strength; Amal, rippling with hormonal energy and angry as hell at the domestic upset his father's 3 a.m. arrivals brought. He wonders now whether he still has the agility and the resilience to hit an old man; to really hurt him.

He remembers the softness of Puppa's cheek, that for some reason it felt softer than when he kissed him; pillow soft; his knuckles springing back from the doughy elasticity of his skin. Sam's genes are far removed from those Indian genomes that mostly shape Joshi faces; round and veering towards chubby. His is square and defined, everything about his obtuseness hanging from razor-sharp cheekbones.

All the tension he's ever felt towards Sam has never reached down as far as his fist, his head and heart absorbing both the little nicks and the general aura of benign tolerance which floats his way. But he sees now that it could happen, and entertains the momentary pleasure it would bring. He is under no illusion that Sam would return the courtesy in such circumstances. Amal carries more weight but his father-in-law has a considerable height advantage, a factor that guarantees he will be knocked out with the return punch. Sam is lean and strong. All that guff about the washing machine was motivated by a desire to see him sweat. So even if Sam does manage to have more sense in the heat of the moment, realizes it is not such a great thing to punch your son-in-law with your complete body strength, even a slap and a demonstrative push in the right position would send him staggering into the ugly bird bath.

How to come back from a descent into physicality? How to face his wife? Is there anything worth bloodying a knuckle for, in the first place?

What ties him to this house aside from the ring on his left hand and a signed certificate curling with damp in their attic? He thinks of the feuds that have run and continue to run across various strands in his family, most of them originating from far lesser slights. Aunts have not spoken to cousins after allegedly being ignored at weddings; brothers have fought over lost tools, or the wills of those still living; sisters-in-law turn mute over stolen recipes and unreturned saris.

As a child, their house dog at his paternal grandparents' in Kolkata, Sunny, needed to be beaten just once by Puppa before he learned never to wolf food from the table again. Perhaps such a lesson is what Sam needs: a firm gesture to end the constant wind-ups, and to ease the stinging still felt in his fingers from having the photograph snatched away.

But he knows how weak a plunge into fighting will make him: chaiwalla trying to stand his ground three years too late. The time has passed to mark his territory.

If he wanted respect he should have commanded it from the outset. Like Sunny, pissing in a corner of their living room on the day they brought him home.

Sam's body language too has changed – he has stiffened, his frame defensively hunched, eyes narrowed, lips pursed into little more than a slit. His fingers tighten and slacken into his palm as if warming up. He has been showing signs of developing arthritis in his hands. Amal know this, but only wants to read warfare into his gestures, like re-enacting historical battles they're so fond of doing in this part of the world. Crusader vs. Raj.

'Where's this shouting come from, son? They'll hear us inside.'

'Tell me what you see!'

'Sun gone to your head or something? You're acting very strangely.'

'Stop detracting and answer the question.'

'Perhaps your blood sugar is low. I've some fruit pastilles in the greenhouse.'

'It's not the damn sugar.'

'Dehydrated, then. I read somewhere that too much tea has a diuretic effect.'

'Piss off.'

'What's going on, Amal? Is the hole upsetting you? She used to do this all the time, I told you. Nothing to worry about. Just those pregnant hormones flying around.'

Sam has political qualities, this ability to slip free from

arguments, something he has never fully appreciated. Even in the face of a knuckle sandwich lies Sam's proven belief that he can talk himself out of anything.

'You smell funny, the pair of you.'

Doorstep interrogation; without satisfactory answers no man shall pass.

'I took our boy on a little investigation, love. We found more holes in the garden.'

'He'd better not have got you drinking. It's the brewery smell you've brought back with you. Or should that be, the distillery smell.'

'I could say the same for you.'

Her laugh is incredulous; acidic in its commentary.

'Nice try, Samuel, but my breath comes from the Herald as you well know. From the old WI speciality: tea laced with Sloe Gin. But you, mister, I know what you're like when you start fiddling inside that shed. Start confusing the homebrew with the workbench. I'm going to need a hand with dinner in the next couple of hours and you're already half cut.'

In rare alcohol-induced instances they still unknowingly strive to make him feel the outsider. It is the three of them who cluster around the backdoor frame, yet she only addresses Sam, harking back to an earlier conjugal role, when young visitors needed to be admonished for being bad influences.

This is perhaps the third such time when Liz has dealt with him in this way – the earlier occasions being pre-marriage, when rudeness could be written-off as a parental sizing-up – but he feels it just as acutely.

He and Claud have never argued this way, before an audience. Their rows are staged in cars and across mobiles. She has been bred differently, to flare up as and when things happen, but he trained himself to save it; absorb her anger, irritation like a shock absorber until they could go at it hammer and tongs somewhere private. He loves her too much to see her unravel in public. That's *his* upbringing. They have no idea how much he protects their daughter from following her parental steps. No bloody idea.

'You disappeared for a while at the Herald, didn't you? I thought you'd gone home at one point.'

'That sugary tea gave me a headache. I'm not used to it.'

'I looked everywhere.'

'Went to walk it off. I'm sorry.'

Liz finds little in his answers that is satisfactory. Eyes him as suspiciously as she did the first time he was brought home. Veils of courtesy in progressively lighter deniers. Aware that she's nodding affirmatively even though she still thinks him same as other men: capable of straightforward lying.

'Oh, that's fine. I'm actually preoccupied with something else now, namely why my daughter is dressed like one of the Three Degrees? The last time she wore Long was at your honeymoon breakfast, and that was like pulling teeth.'

'I hadn't noticed.'

'What's been going on in that house of yours this week?'

Throughout this exchange, Sam stands by her side and clears his throat in a series of nervous tics. In a reversal of their campaigning personas, domestically at least, Liz is the one to be relied upon to lead the charge. Bouddicea in tan corduroy. Daughter welfare, forward! While Sam's power lies in debate – stubborn logic descending into flummoxed, snappy nastiness – he lacks the empathy needed to cluster round the Aga. The discomfort shows in his face, not happy to have raised voices within the home; within Claud's earshot.

'You're all my little honeybees,' he had said once, on detecting Amal's resistance at one of the earliest dinners, when a Sussex sleepover and a Sunday morning church visit were mandatory if he was to succeed in winning them over. 'There's nothing I like more than when we're all buzzing together.'

Liz crosses her arms tightly, impatient for his answer. Her posture harks back to a quarter century prior: Mum at the school gate readying herself to sort out another playground dispute.

'I-I-I . . .'

'Out with it, Amal. I know there's something she's not telling me.'

From the corner of his eye he can see Sam blinking some kind of warning. Embattled husbands must stand together; a show of allegiance he hadn't anticipated.

'She's been feeling low for the past couple of days. The doctor said to expect it. Crash after a high, and everything. I've been coming home to tears most night this week.'

'Ah! The dreaded hormones! That explains it.'

'Don't sound so pleased about it, Samuel. Pregnancy's hard enough to cope with as it is, without having your emotions boomeranging all over the place.'

'The dressing-up's probably helping her, Liz. Making her feel better about herself.'

'Yes, you're right, of course Amal. It just made me stop in my tracks for a moment when I saw her. Just not the sort of think I'd imagine her doing.'

As Liz computes this her face softens; a mother relenting on a hapless son. Making the most of what has been given to her through marriage.

'Like you said, pregnancy makes you do the strangest things. I'm just finding this out for myself.'

'Better fasten your seat belt, mate. You have no idea what's lying ahead. If she's anything like my good lady wife here, you're in for some fun and games.'

He offers tea; a peacekeeper, trying to dampen down hostility across all sides. Two cups each, with lots of sugar, thaws the chill in some areas and sobers up others. Now there is peace in the house, persuading them to go letter-boxing with a stack of remaining loose leaflets in order to keep up the momentum of interest from the Herald. That there are five further boxes in the utility room waiting for similarly eager readers is not his problem. They can be dropped at the libraries and the shops in and around Lewes early next week.

His father-in-law is a fervent believer in an Englishman's home being his castle; happy to employ all these clichés about nationality. This is half the reasoning behind the leaflets in the first place; to defend his precious beautiful castle until his last breath – either in his sleep or when a burglar slips a window catch and twists one of Liz's steak knives into his chest cavity.

The old village traditions still stand. So long as someone is home or in the immediate area all the doors stay unlocked until ten thirty. Tense teenagers aside, the most that has been taken from the house in thirty years of them living there is a golfing umbrella from the porch, and half a bag of sugar when the WI meeting next door ran short.

Similarly, he knows that the cars will also be unlocked; both the Range Rover and more importantly the boot of Liz's hatchback, the alarm off, waiting for his hands to push the catch and release the washing machine clogging up its insides. If he can plumb the washing machine without them catching on (how, with his clumsy coordination and cluelessness with domestic appliances?), he feels he can win some vital point against Sam, delineating an area of skill where only he reigns supreme. Fathers-to-be need to know this stuff. They cannot raise children who think that they are useless on all practical fronts.

The child they might one day have, will have, must never feel at a loss, unprepared to handle the notion of strength, when only brute strength is needed. Whether boy or girl, he has to ensure that they are raised to be both physically fit and intelligent. From a young age, the first age that it is safe to do so, they will be given cardiovascular training and set loose on the small weights. By the time they start high school they will have the brains of geniuses and the bodies of athletes. They will love their parents and not be afraid of anything.

In the grip of tense, outstretched arms, the washing machine feels lighter than he imagines, its move achievable, until its full weight becomes apparent once it is free from the depths of the boot, with only its merest edge resting along the rear bumper. Brown hands on white goods. The irony does not escape him. He feels he should take a picture and stick it on the shelf in the living room along with the others. Marriage equals modern-day slavery.

Moving it as far as he has, five yards in a series of jagged, grunt-powered pulls, not overtly worrying about the effects of a bumpy trajectory upon the machine's delicate drum mechanism, has used up all his reserves. Until he recalls the trolley sitting in the shed and goes to pick the padlock. He remembers too reading somewhere how at concerts singer pep up their energy by snacking on strips of cooked chicken during costume changes. He would do the same if Claud could be called down. But she is having another catnap before tea, the garden-digging and cake-making wearying her to a similar degree.

He has not yet spoken to her about the time capsules. He does not want to embarrass her. Better to monitor her response as he tramps outside her window, an attention-seeking teenager tortured with unrequited love, as he stamps the mud from his shoes, heels clicking against flagstones in a loud, aggressive quick-march. A shadow floats behind the Victorian glass but it could just as easily be curtains.

He is unsure of her presence until the washing machine slips first from the trolley's rusted bumper and consequently from his grasp, dropping onto the drive with a thick, polystyrene-insulated slap. There is no drama attached to the noise, but the echoing ring of the drum rattling inside its tin cage is enough to bring her to the window proper. Her face is sleepy – everything to remember about this day will be based around her readily falling into unconsciousness as if nothing about his presence in the real world, his support, is worth staying awake for – her eyes understanding the spontaneity of his latest tangent.

In spite of the ringing that courses through his body with the shock of the sudden drop, like an inner spring that refuses to settle, he shrugs off his cack-handed effort and waves up to her. She does not respond, simply content to observe, something in the slight incline of her head indicating an appraisal of some kind, as if he is a mating bull being paraded in the ring at market. To buy or not to buy?

'It's my turn to surprise them,' he calls, his voice cracking with fake cheerfulness, 'think they'll be pleased?'

'You shouldn't waste your time,' she mouths. 'Nothing you do will make any difference.'

He squints through the late-afternoon sunlight to see her better, understanding that the furrow across his eyebrows give him a studious look, masking his sense of panic, his inner spring powering back to high-jump. Bungee jump. He has to be able to make a difference. If not, he has no business being there.

She continues to stand at the window, expressionless as the glass; a blank.

'Hold on. I'm coming up.'

He will not allow this to happen. He will not give up. It has taken longer than he thought, a night and most of the day, but a state of shock has finally emerged within her. All the sleep she's had has given her the energy to play dead.

As he runs up the stairs he fears he will be unable to

cover the lifelessness that lies behind her eyes, knowing that Liz will immediately detect the sinking of her girl; sniff the lost baby in seconds. The trouble he can handle; what he cannot face is the possibility of having to articulate their grief on his own.

Of all the rooms in the house it is perhaps Claud's bedroom where he feels the most uncomfortable. Liz tried to move them into one of the larger guest rooms after they were married as a gentle suggestion that childish things should be left in childhood. But Claud stubbornly sticks to the back room that overlooks the garden, barely large enough to hold the double bed, wardrobe and dresser. What it holds in its favour is the evening light that streams though the triple window panels. He understands how a bad day at sixth form can be made better by letting the sunlight smooth out the worst of a teenager's angst.

Each time he steps over the threshold he sees Claud in her younger incarnation, wilful and argumentative. Messy. Even now, he sees the tangled bedclothes, and how her shoes have been thrown over the bed at the back wall, probably the same spot where she dumped them as a girl. Tidy Claud, who likes everything in Richmond to be in its place, drops her coat to the floor; lets the contents of her bag spill onto the bed. Sleeps on top of her make-up bag without it being a problem. Even her posture is different, hunched and defensive. Her body language is asking for a fight.

Also, the same bed where younger, more energetic boyfriends have made their mark. He has none of their daring. In their place he is moved to paralysis, pretending to fall asleep.

Ignoring his unease he puts his arms around her, the strength in the crook of his elbow and in his hands killing her wriggling, squirming movements, as she jerks her body like a fish fighting for its last breath. He will absorb her fight. Squeeze the life back into her. Make her aware of the world and that they have a place in it.

'You shouldn't get so close to me. I'm defective.'

The more she tries to fight him the tighter he holds her. Bone to bone. Hoping the friction will act as a kind of muffler, absorbing the words she shouldn't be saying.

'You'll catch it too. No woman will want you.'

If there was a pillow to hand, closer than at the other end of the room, he would place it over her mouth to stop her speaking. His hand alone is no good. Each time he tries to cover her she spits on his palm. Hot, flaming spit drawn from the hatred that sits in her gut. The pillow would be a better silencer, allowing her to concentrate on her breathing and to melt into the physical wall of shoulder and chest.

He wants her to understand that is what support should feel like, crushing, and all encompassing. Instead, he has to contend with her effort to impress upon him the key component of her deterioration; a husk with a voice. Her eyes continuously scrambling in explanation, vehemently, indignantly, as if she is in the dock protesting her innocence against trumped-up charges.

Her eyes frighten him more than her speech, unsettling him as they dart around, dark, free of restraint and roving like a mad woman. Her frame feels brittle within his hands.

There is no chance of her melding into him and taking shelter against the wall. Compassion will not reach her. Nor will stronger measures work. A sound shaking will not be felt. Three hours ago he could have communicated with her, made some reference to the time capsules at least. Show he understood. Now he is not so sure. She is too deep in a spiral for him to pull her out.

He goes back to the washing machine when he sees how useless it is, the heat of the struggle stinging the tops of his ears. Everywhere else he is as cold as ice, frozen with failure. She cannot be pacified unless she is left alone to torture herself. This is what she wants.

Maybe the only magic he can find comes from insensitivity. Spite.

'You're parents will be back in forty minutes. That's how long you've got to pull yourself together. Don't embarrass me.'

He batters the cold water pipe in a tidal stream of bitterness. A series of hard, fast thwacks that bring out the tendons in his forearm. Clanks of metal on metal echo dangerously under the counter tops. He is uncertain whether he is bashing his head in or Claud's. All he knows is the simple relief he feels for imagining serious cranial damage to someone; cracking a skull like a boiled egg and allowing the steam to escape.

'Hello, matey. I seem to be knocking on air here. Think the local cider has turned me invisible, or something.'

The man at the kitchen door is not one he recognizes at first. Same age as him; same kind of clothes. It takes a moment for the accent to register: France via several years in South London. A newer stranger in village than him and still he feels foolish, aware of how his spanner-anger must have seemed to an onlooker.

'Looks like you're engaging in some serious manual labour there, buddy. I'm the same with DIY myself. Half an hour with a T-bolt and I have the same rages.'

The acceptance of his anger as solid fact is anything but British, and brings his spanner-arm to a halt. One after the other they give wordless shrugs of solidarity, but in his gut he wishes the Frenchman to be like the rest of them. As with the café staff, he is not ready for people to be nice to him; does not wish to let down his guard.

He wonders whether this is the beginning of the shift, where Claud gets stronger whilst he becomes weaker, unable to interact with anybody.

'You must be the famous printer. My in-laws have been singing your praises all afternoon. I'm Amal, by the way.'

He offers his hand as both introduction and apology.

'Phil. Good to meet you finally. I've heard great things.'

His hand and wrist are being gripped in a double handshake, firm, sincere, with friendliness he wasn't expecting, causing him to back away towards the safety of the washing machine. He sees the blush rising from his neck glow against the clinical, unforgiving white.

'I saw your handiwork earlier. The flyers? Good job.'

'Thanks. Took a couple of attempts but we got there in the end.'

Phil leans casually against the back counter, hip resting on the drawer handle, with a familiarity that suggests that he is no stranger to this kitchen. He has visions of Sam holding court from the coffee percolator. Not kitchen-table activism, but important creative summits, with the poor wretched flyers going through five to ten drafts before reaching the final printing stage.

'We're almost there, lad. Just a couple of small changes and we're there. Small changes, that's all. So we get it absolutely right. But while we're at it, we might take a look at those other blues you were talking about for the borders. This one doesn't look right at all . . .'

'I've just come to drop the bill. I can leave it with you if that's ok.'

'Sure,' he says, adopting the casualness because they are buddies now. He can see Phil becoming an ally in this part of the world: drinking partners in the village pub, talking over the Sunday broadsheets to convince themselves that they still have city dust in their bones.

'We had a road-block at the Herald this afternoon. You should have seen it, Phil. They gobbled them up. Snatching them out of our hands like nobody's business.'

They both laugh at the truth of that; Amal's, nervous and agreeable, Phil's long and slow, as laid-back as his posture.

'I'm sure that made Sam very happy. Keep the illegal folks in Calais and let my French brothers deal with them.'

'Sounds like you know him very well already.'

'Oh! Where's my manners, I should be saying congratulations, shouldn't I, matey? He offers his hand again, a sign that he has assimilated everything that is cricket and above board. 'You won't have time to tinker about with washing machines when your tiny feet arrive.'

'They told you?'

His voice hardens more than he means it to, but it is too late to add any warmth once the words have escaped his lips.

In a village where neighbours know each other's business, the fact that it is everyone — milkman, postman, and now, printer — is too much to swallow. The idea that he cannot walk across the Green and not be accosted, buy a paper from the local shop or sit in church without pairs of knowing, sympathetic eyes following him, levels his skewed spirit.

This is why he can never live here; to stand aside and let

his hard-earned freedoms be curtailed. How their ears will burn from village talk if they do. The barren couple with the lovely house and no children to fill it.

Once Claud is in the car tonight, he will drive and keep driving until they are taken into the city's concrete arms. He will do his level best to stay away, think up any excuse, until he can feel like a stranger to them; a myth. This is the only way he can hold his head up. He is prepared to break Claud's heart, and Liz's and Sam's, to make it happen.

Phil frowns in puzzlement, the first crack in an otherwise perfect demeanour.

'I'm sorry, matey. I didn't understand it was like that. I was just doing some work for them. They thought it was right to tell me in the circumstances.'

The parental broadcasting, like the pregnancy itself, gone rogue and out of his control.

'I'm sorry too, mate, but it's our news to share. Nothing personal. Seems like half the village knew before we did, almost.'

This virulent anger that flushes from his ears and deep into his chest should have been deployed when he was being toasted on the Green earlier in the afternoon. Only then he was chicken, reduced to spineless, simpering gestures. Too busy stuffing himself with stale cake to raise any significant objection.

One on one is different, however. One on one he can

handle. He showed Sam, didn't he? Raised his voice and laid his territory. It should be no different with this guy, friendly innocent or not.

They are both aware that the initial fraternity has darkened, though the strength of Amal's malicious intent is bleached out by the renewed strength of the late-afternoon light. He is not jealous of physical types – too easy a shot – nor is he so insecure to be disabled by the toned, muscular presence standing close to the doorway.

A man as easy on the eye as Phil is not perfect, but he knows how to keep it simple. Where is the sorrow in those long, loose limbs; the summer-house tan; the boyish hair, and perfectly straight teeth? If anything he needs something of what this guy has: confidence; certainty. He wants to retrieve the ability to look Claud in the eye and speak with conviction, rather than this dance of downward eyes and verbal stumbling blocks.

They need escape, some California sunshine to reduce their pain to mere blight; a blip. They need tanned skin and clinically white teeth to hide their worry and regain some of their promise. Need red string bands around their wrists to ward off bad spirits, to convince themselves that everything happens for a reason. They need to believe in something, even if it is just the bare strands of their marriage.

'You must excuse me if I'm acting like an idiot,' he says finally. 'My concentration's been taken up with this thing. I needed to take it out on somebody.'

'No need to explain, matey. You should see me when I've got my head stuck inside a carbon cartridge. I don't come up for days.'

'Can I get you a drink or something? Liz will never forgive me if she hears you called and I didn't offer you anything.'

But a trace of flint still remains in his tone, suggesting a cup laced with poison, tea garnished with flob. He wonders if a return to the placid can ever be possible after this.

'No, it's fine. You've got enough on your plate by the look of it. Unless of course, you're looking for an extra pair of hands.'

'I don't. Thanks.'

Manners regained, but he's curt with it. If a promise of friendship ever existed, an escape from insular in-laws, a like-minded mate who could be as loyal as Hari, it is now lost. No matter. He has better things to be doing: punishing himself with the kitchen-work, making up with his wife.

After Phil has gone, he tears open the envelope left on the counter top. He needs to know how much Sam can afford to piss away on local bugbears at the expense of his future grandchild. Two thousand flyers design and print: £500. One hundred grandparent-shower invitations: £250.

Samples of each enclosed of which one interests Amal:

We're having a baby!

We thought we'd waved goodbye to the sleepless nights and the nappy bin, and look what's happened!

You are cordially invited to attend our Grandparent-shower to celebrate Claud and Amal's forthcoming arrival, next Saturday at 3 p.m.

This is a celebration of all things Grandparent. Silver foxes and HRT patches welcome.

Kid-free zone! Plenty of booze! RSVP

Footsteps as he continues to bust his bollocks with the plumbing; light-footed, apologetic. And he had thought shifting the washing machine itself was the hard part, struggling to take the weight from the trolleys, taking care not to scrape the white rubber wheels against the gravel outside, and protecting the re-varnished kitchen floor inside. In keeping everything pristine, his brogues have taken the brunt of it, the leather across each toe cap gnarled and bashed-in. The yard is also the recipient of his frustration, littered with jettisoned plastic wrap and broken-up polystyrene. Small, almost triangular, piles of detached white crumbs make it appear as though synthetic snowfall has settled on the patio; an industrial winter wonderland to decimate all mention of the Herald of Spring.

He continues to be motivated by failure. Every misplaced effort of the day has led to this moment, stretching his left hand to breaking as he grapples to connect the cold water lead to the tap socket in an under-counter space only suited for a small child. If there is a simpler way to do things, he is not aware of it. All he knows is that the day will not be wasted if he does this one small thing. This one fiddly thing.

Aware of the clock working against him, he ignores the sharp pang he feels across his tendons as he twists the plastic stopper over the tap using thumb and forefinger. He needs to vacuum the outside mess and to make everything pretty before they return.

He does not turn to look at her until he is certain that the lead is secure and not liable to break free from the tap under the pressure of running water. It has taken him twenty minutes to get to this point, during which time his anger has only amplified. Anything she wants to say will have to wait.

'Perfect timing. Give me a hand with the broom if you're up to it?'

'That was a bastard thing to say, upstairs. You wouldn't have dared say that if there was anyone else in the house.'

She has changed into something that makes her look less volatile: jeans and one of Sam's Aran jumpers.

'If I was angry enough, I would.'

'No, you wouldn't. You're too weak.'

Anything can happen in this house: photos can be buried; wounds twisted open. Also, the freedom to shout, from not having to worry about what the neighbours will think. He replays the tone in his head, patronizing and designed to hurt. Knows it is one never used at home, where their tempers are as manicured as the topiary on the front step; where one is happy to creep around the other. Explosions only ever seem to happen in the car – something about the combustibility of the engine activates their intolerance mechanisms – or here.

'You didn't seem to be hearing me. I didn't know what else to do. I read somewhere that speaking sharply can bring people out of uncommunicative states.'

'You're pathetic.'

'What happened is no one's fault, Claud. The doctor said . . .'

'I was there, thank you. It wasn't my hearing that was lost, just . . . something else.'

'Claud . . .'

'He feels calling me a geriatric will make his explanation clearer. I'm thirty-four. In whose world does that make me a geriatric?'

She may as well have never read the pile of books that sat on her bedside table. As if poring over pages and pages of the stuff in the last year had prepared her for nothing.

'It's only a medical term. You know that. They have to have some basis of classification otherwise how can they be expected to know how to treat everyone?'

'Thanks for that, 'Mal. You're doing a really good job of making me feel better.'

He cannot rise to her challenge to crush her to powder. He will not destroy her by saying what is on his mind. He was meaning to be helpful in his tone. The doctor's explanation had little to cling onto, but there were threads . . . and if she was disbelieving in the threads, hard medical facts, why did they go the hospital in the first place?

'I've connected the washing machine. A couple of final pushes and it'll be in place.'

'No one's going to be placated with a Bosche, 'Mal. They'd rather have a grandchild over clean clothes.'

'They're going to get a grandchild. Just a little later than they think.'

'In your dreams. I'm dead in the water. I can feel it.'

'We're not giving up.'

'You can be as hopeful as you like. It's not going to happen.'

She says what he is thinking: that this is it. Their one chance blown. It is the stark finality of the decision that has been thundering in his chest, he realizes, not the rising panic on how quickly her mood has changed.

What are they doing wanting children in the first place? When did they both agree that this was the right thing to do?

There were plenty of comments made at the wedding by both sets of relatives, and from friends with brats of their own; fraudulently selling the dream the way hawkish dealers push timeshares onto the weak and uncertain. On a day that looked forward to a happy and fulfilled future, these friends pounced on the unequivocal hope in their eyes, with a carefully choreographed presentation of tidily dressed, cake-filled children, adorable and exceptionally behaved. The little monsters were their show homes, high-spirited, lightly argumentative, but essentially perfect. Who would not want to be in the market to buy after that?

The hustling was to be expected. A biologically geriatric bride and groom shuffling towards the marriage bed whilst there was still enough opportunity for sluggish eggs and weak sperm to fuse and root down; begin life. But they had never had that specific conversation. Never sat on the sofa, or in bed, or anywhere else, to discuss why the actual mixing of their genes needed to be brought into the world. Did they think about other ways of addressing the emptiness: hobbies where they spent more time together; a dog? Everything about the collection of cells had been implicit. Their eyes lied, so they read the need in each other's body language. Even when it felt like they were at their closest, physically all-consuming, somewhere, in the crook of an arm, a cavity in their pumping hearts, was a final gap waiting to be filled.

So at the wedding, she looked at the show homes and lapped it up with a never-ending thirst. He was put on a diet as soon as they returned from honeymoon.

'You don't mean that. It's still the shock talking.'

Fears can be banished. Difficult, near-impossible procedures tried again. Medical assistance can be sought. Money paid. He no longer believes what has been running through his head since he saw the burial box in the garden: that there is no place in the world for a meeting of the Sussex and Kolkata gene. He wants a child with Claud more than anything. It is the natural order of things.

'All these books I've read. Months reading these books. And I'm still not prepared for how shitty I feel.'

'Books can't teach you everything, Claud. Don't apologize for the way you're feeling.'

This will pass. Like the way she stands with her back to the door ready to run if he tries to touch her; the pinkness around the eyes, raw and inflamed, telling of the battle raging in the space behind there; the twist he feels in his cheeks from keeping his mouth straight, avoiding both its crumble into tears and a sometime desire to let rip and curse everything that lives, including his wife. All things will pass.

Their baby has gone. Someone somewhere is to blame: a rogue blood cell or free radical; bacteria from food. An external factor: sudden motion such a lift shuddering when it should not have, or an idiot at the supermarket not watching where he was going and bumping her trolley. Her body has reacted to a previous action. That much is certain. Now, he realizes, he needs to find out what it was.

There is silence all the way to the pub, but one that is comfortable, as if, whilst an understanding is still a long way off, there is at least the possibility of a stalemate. They will not tear chunks out of one another. She will not stare at him with hatred for not having a body that can hold a child; he will try and look at her without apportioning blame.

The pub is dead aside from a scattering of old men drinking alone around the bar. The Herald has finished everyone else off. An atmosphere of weariness pervades the village. Even the trees in the car park bow their heads, exhausted.

They take a table where they won't be disturbed or have to socialize. Again they share a tacit agreement in this. Claud has paid no attention to the head-count, walking blankly though a succession of glazed doors that lead to the Snug, as if it was reserved solely for their purpose. Amal remains spatially aware, looking to see whether he recognizes any of the soaks from the afternoon's festivities, or if they have been rooted to the same spot since opening; they too looking for a place to hide.

Alcohol loosens them a little. In the past, they would cosy up on the cushioned love seat against the window, if not loved-up, then at least in minor thrall to one another. Hands casually resting on thighs, fingers brushing cheeks and the side of necks. Tired of conception sex perhaps, but still aware of the magnetism of the other's body. The force of the magnetic pull outweighing freshly realized tics, flaws and other disappointments. Now she sits alone on the love seat. He takes a stool and places it opposite; the round, high table between them giving further protection. A border for their personal space.

She has not taken off her coat. He toys with the rim of his half-pint glass.

'We can't be out too long. They'll be wondering where we are.'

'You needed a drink.'

'We have drinks at home.'

'You know what I mean. Besides, I left a post-it. They'll probably join us before long.'

She looks around in appraisal, as if the place is new to her; sips her red wine with distaste.

'So this is the new theory, is it? Getting drunk makes everything better?'

'It can do. You're from the Home Counties. You should be well practiced.'

'That's the second bastard thing you've said today. Don't know what's got into you this afternoon. You've been acting strange ever since you got back from the Herald.'

'You're one to talk. Shut up and finish your drink.'

'Shut up and finish yours. It's bitter, not a bloody cocktail.'

They laugh a little because the nagging seems so normal;

a flashback to three days ago; three weeks ago; a couple of hours after they met.

'This is going to send me loopy. I'm still taking the painkillers they gave me for the cramps.'

'You're still cramping?'

'The body doesn't stop just because the baby's not there. Do you know anything about my physiognomy apart from the bits that help you get your rocks off?'

'That's not fair.'

'Why is it I seem to know everything about how your body functions and you know nothing about mine?'

'I was only asking because you hadn't mentioned it before. Someone discharged themselves on their own. I lost my opportunity to ask any questions.'

'There's the internet. You could have been using the internet instead of standing around with your mouth open.'

'You think I've had time for the internet? Now you're the one who's in another world.'

There was a great vision they had for themselves. That their forties would be fatter and all the more contented for having a brood getting under their feet. Things would not always be easy, but at the very least there would be a couple of bare, harmonious strands holding them together. Like his parents. Hers. Now he does not see how they will get there at all.

Pubs are her environment, not his. A country girl, she

has been brought up in them; in this very one, in fact. Church, school, social centre, dating service and crisis support all housed under a modernized coaching inn. She should command presence here. The banquette should not need to support her back, in place of the iron rod that usually bears her. If anything, she looks frailer than before; the drink softening her into a rag, crumpled and ready to fade into the background, like furniture, inanimate and static.

'You don't want to be here, do you?'

'Here's as good as anywhere else.'

'I'm sorry. I thought it would cheer you up.'

'Cheer me up? This isn't a bad day at the office. Or is it, to you?'

'No. I don't know. Just wanted to do something that made you happy. Relaxed, at least.'

'It's going to take a long time before that happens so be prepared.'

He wants to shout that she has not prepared him for anything. The books have stayed in her domain. Her side of the bed. Everything he has been told has been on a need to know. Aware of how feeble that makes him sound, weaker than a girl with a sofa for a spine, he keeps his mouth shut. Aware too how the corners of his eyes crease heavily when he breaks into ineffectual protestation. She has hectored him enough times about its unattractiveness and instant ageing qualities.

Limbo dominates. He has been in freefall because he has lacked structure and the influence of third parties. What he longs for is a dry old sandwich in the café opposite his office and a lunch hour of talking bullshit with the guys on his team. The two-hour abyss from lunch until tea; then the final two-hour stretch, usually a meeting where he can daydream and count down the minutes until the metaphorical bell rings and the mass descent to the bar.

Free time works only when there is no crisis. He sees no end to this day, nor to the lowering of their postures. Tonight if they fall asleep at all, they will remain hunched, taut, stop and start.

'I didn't mean it. What I said before. Of course I want to try again.'

There is nothing to say. He has to take her lead. He will only open his mouth for beer.

'You got me when I'd just woken up. I'd been thinking about it in my sleep. It frightened me, the thought of what we'd have to go through. Awake, slightly pissed, I feel I can handle it. Raring to go, actually.'

'Is this the right thing to do?'

'As soon as possible. Tonight if we can.'

Under the table, his legs shudder involuntarily at the thought. He will hug but cannot touch her in that way. Needs to be anywhere but. The tension in his jaw resumes. His whole head frozen with it.

Men, Hari says, will fuck anything. If it's on the rag, they'll fuck it; if it's asleep, they'll fuck it; if it has two heads and a mouth like a bag full of spanners, they'll have a go.

He does not know why her words suddenly bring him back to this nasty, bachelor mindset. Perhaps his nervousness. He giggled when Puppa told him his grandfather had died. Same territory; his mind spanning to previously unthinkable tangents. Still, it is disgusting. In his so-called heyday he never got anyone. Never laid claim so indiscriminately the way Hari did. He had too much deference.

Is this what he thinks of his wife? Former pedestal royalty humbled into doggy style in the sewer? To be humiliated in the way of Hari's damaged women? Truth: he wants to hold her, but does not want to lie with her. Comfort her, but not touch her. Revive her, but still forsaking the act.

Maybe she is talking over her truth: that it might be best to call it a day after their one shot failed. No shame in that. Save themselves the heartache, something that will leave deeper scars if, as he is starting to suspect, the next pregnancy goes the way of the first.

He thinks of all the great things that couples can do without the burden of children. How their lives could remain an abundance of spontaneity and disposable income. They could buy a holiday home abroad. Two. One on each hemisphere if that is what would make her happy. He racks his mind to think of the childless couples they know – not the kids from the office; guys their age and older – but cannot dredge any up. In their immediate circle, there are no trailblazers, only conformists. No matter. They are taste makers, she and him. They can set the precedent.

There are all those hotels advertising breaks 'just for adults'. The supermarket shop can be done online. Gyms hit before work. Multiplex cinemas eschewed for Arthouse. Theatre replacing bars and the occasional nightclub. Everything in their life can be tailored, shaded, trimmed to the point where children become like the dodo – rarely sighted, and then finally, extinct.

They can find a way back to sex, just not now. He is not the man to take advantage of the wounded, the dead. These things must come back in their own time no matter how loud her hormonal alarms. He realizes how it will be seen: as the ultimate revenge for being treated like a mating machine, but he cannot help his feelings. He will withhold. He must.

But only in his head is he the leader of anything. Leaning forward, she grabs his forearm and shakes it urgently.

'If we mark a start tonight, we could be pregnant in a few weeks. I won't conceive tonight, I know that. We just have to believe that we can. No one need know.'

He laughs harder than he means to, both incredulous and frightened by her tunnel vision.

'I think they'll work it out when the pregnancy spans ten or eleven months.'

'Some babies stay in the womb past their due date. What were you telling me about your cousin's wife?'

'She was three weeks late. But she was also obese. The sprog had to push through all the fat. Why do you care what people think all of a sudden? When our kid comes it'll be the right time. Call it destiny, it doesn't sound too mystical. Nothing to do with fear of losing face, looking stupid.'

He is harsher than he needs to be. Hates himself for it, the pain that crinkles her forehead; the determined shake that banishes it away. The hand that retreats from its place on his arm back to the fold of her lap. Wounded crustacean, preyed upon, crawling back to its shell.

Someone has to be logical. Show leadership. This is probably what they advise in the counselling leaflets they left behind at the hospital. They can give in to their imaginations but not to fantasy. Nothing good can come of such indulgence. As the husband, it is down to him to be the tough guy. No one else can be trusted to give her these firm truths.

He will be the captain of their ship, sailing with a steady hand. There will be a need for steadfastness but he will be fair with it, just until the waters settle and she sees that desperation is not the route they need to take. Thirty-four may not be the same as twenty-four, but they still have all the time in the world if they can keep their heads.

'Please 'Mal. Please, let's do this.'

The steel in her eyes ready to level him to dust. The note in her pleading, chills. It promises harmful consequences if he does not adhere. Unable to hold her gaze he goes to the bar. Let the alcohol flood the desperation out of her. Wash the need away.

He downs a double whiskey chaser at the bar whilst waiting for his pint, not caring whether or not she notices. She has had the luxury of sleeping pills. He needs this. Usually he would turn to face her whilst the bar girl is getting the drinks together, both of them indulging in this distant perspective on the other; seeing how strangers might see them. Not today. That he feels her crumbling in her seat is enough.

The shot puts him on the wrong side of sober. He is a sorry excuse for a husband. An overnight stay at Liz and Sam is no longer a flight of fancy, but a necessity; once he gets to the bottom of that pint glass a very obvious one. No matter. There are greater things to worry over.

She has moved to a new table in the centre of the room where he must join her. Here stools take preference over chairs, as if her intention is to force them both to rediscover their backbone. She sits dead straight in a Finishing School posture. In Sussex they learn these rules almost by osmosis. He puts a fresh glass in her hand, noticing now that the old one remains barely touched on the other table.

'Two forty.'

'What?'

'I've been doing some mental arithmetic. Two hundred and forty.'

'I don't get you.'

'You realize I've been having periods since I was fourteen? Twenty years of it. Twenty times twelve. That's two hundred and forty opportunities to have a baby and almost every one of those passed up.'

'You have to stop this, Claud. You're not being fair on yourself.'

'This has nothing to do with feeling sorry for myself. I'm stating biological facts. I've had over two hundred chances and I ignored them. What's that they say about listening to your body? It's true, isn't it?'

'We have jobs that we love . . .'

'Trust you to make it worse than it already is. My career's to blame, is it?'

Through the muddle of alcohol, he is still flooded with a sweet sense of familiarity. These are traps he regularly falls in, where he stitches himself up with thoughtless attempts at empathy. He says the wrong thing whether she has had a bad day at work or been short changed at the dry cleaner. Nothing can be the matter if they are treading down these well-worn paths. He is comfortable in this province of trip-ups and hashed apologies. Quells the fear of earlier when everything was uncharted, unexplained.

'I've said it wrong, as usual.'

'If I'd have given in that night of the Christmas Fayre. Dropped my knickers instead of giving him a hand job.'

'I'm sorry. I should learn to listen more.'

'I could be the mother of a sixteen-year-old child.'

'I've missed something. Who are you talking about?'

'That guy at my sixth form who wanted to burn down Battle. Rory. Wasn't just the Castle he was into.'

He takes her hands, the first time all day, he realizes. Cups them to his lips. It is the closest he'll get to kissing her on the brow, cheeks, mouth.

'You can't keep torturing yourself like this, Claud. What you're talking about is just mathematics. It doesn't have any relevance to real life.'

'Who are you to say what's real to me?'

Outrage in her eyes, but no power to her voice.

'You never had one hundred and fifty chances to get pregnant, or whatever it was. You're a flesh-and-blood woman, not a sodding battery chicken or breeding heifer.'

A flash of a smile: bitter, powered by guilt.

'This from your plan to cheer me up, is it?'

'Look around this place. We've had some good times here, haven't we?'

She has danced on this floor with her shoes off. The soles of her feet blackened with dirt and, before the smoking ban, fag butts. Toes caked with broken crisps and other stray bits of food. Every milestone leading to her thirty-four years has been marked with a loosely choreographed shimmy, same as everyone else who has bred here.

They have danced on this floor together. With abandon. His first Christmas away from Leicester, enjoying the freedom but riddled with nerves; and her, face reddened with a mulled wine and Bacardi mix, seeking to lead him out of it.

She rooted through the catalogue of CDs on the jukebox and pulled up the song from *Dirty Dancing*. One moment he had gone for a piss. The next, she was singing to him across the bar, enthusiastically, tunelessly, until there was no choice but to be Patrick Swayze to her Baby. Groins in step but feet out of kilter. Laughing the whole time. Unable to believe she liked that mushy crap. Cheers from their side of the Snug, as her mates willed them along.

That was their wedding, there. Not the stiff afternoon eight months later both painfully aware of the cost and trying to fool the other out of their self-consciousness. But that moment on the makeshift dance floor was boozy, sweaty perfection. The whole village was in on their bubble; approving of and championing their hope. A perfect start to that Christmas. First of many. Bloody brilliant.

How he has got her dancing, he does not know. There was no power in his suggestion, softly spoken and burdened with compromise. Still, here she is on her feet, holding onto him as they move in a tight space circling the tables.

There is reticence over a full embrace. Instead, they are joined loosely; able to separate at the first sign of the slightest misstep. He is too scared to tempt fate on the jukebox so they dance along to the radio: an urban ballad neither is familiar with but which succeeds in making them feel old. Their moves are silent and awkward. Two cousins at a wedding forced together after accusations of being spoilsports.

Claud nods towards the girl at the bar, preferable to making eye contact with him.

'Bren will think we're a pair of nutters.'

'She's gone to change the barrel. We'll have some privacy for a bit. Anyway, she's not going to mind, so long as I get another round in. Probably seen worse.'

Claud looks for confirmation before continuing. Peers through the clear border of the frosted glass panels that separates the Snug from the rest of the bar. Brenda has disappeared. The information should relax her, but does not. Same as the drink; untouched. Still dances as a pupil, stiff as a board.

'I'd rather be sitting down. If someone comes in I'll feel even more stupid than I already do.'

'Uh-uh. Stay on your feet. Till the song finishes, at least.'

Couples should slow dance, even if they cannot bear to touch one another. Her hold is barely a grasp, as if his shoulder is burning paper; without substance. Her face, downward and studious as she follows his feet, followed by a tense nod, distracted and insular, after noticing their body positioning. He too realizes his mistake, twisting his body a fraction, so that their torsos are at an angle, ballroom-style, rather than touching. He wants to pull something out of her without making her uncomfortable. But he is clumsy and unsuccessful, as if confirming that he too finds her disgusting.

'Just until this song's over, yeah? Too much makes me dizzy.'

She speaks through her teeth, every word as tortuous at the steps.

'Sure. Whenever you like.'

When she told him the news three weeks ago, his first impulse had been to pull her off the sofa in delight. They danced to what was playing at the time, the theme tune to a soap opera followed by an advert for a building society.

'We did it! God knows how, 'Mal, but we did it!'

Laughing then, breathless with the wonder of it. Carelessly spilling their joy in the direction of the make-believe on television. Taking her by surprise, him too, he twirled her round several times to screaming, cheering, elation. They could afford to be that generous with their happiness. In that moment there was more than enough to go around.

Twirls morphed to a cuddle-dance, still giggling breathlessly like schoolchildren who had been told of an imminent treat. Their moves were an amplification of all the bliss they had ever known: the pleasure and then the greediness of Christmas and birthdays, first date, first kiss, first shag, passing exams, getting wasted at the very same Glastonbury, first year at their respective universities, driving down to the coast mid-summer, plugging into people power at raves, slipping back into parental homes at dawn, the first corporate pay packet, sunbathing on hired catamarans, knocking back aperitifs on a pensione terrace, that moment on their wedding night when everyone had finally cleared off and they sat in bed scoffing the remains of the cake.

The cha-cha-cha around the TV was qualified to rank in that scale, though it towered above all else: the Nth Power of pleasure and high-fives; something beyond simple personal gratification. In between catching his breath he saw the same realization reflected in the depth of her eyes, punctuated by brief, acknowledged flashes of fear. She blinked a delicious heart-stopping fear that spoke for both of them. The focus of their meticulous planning, and her belligerent hectoring, was finally real.

They were no longer dancing a couple, newlyweds, boyfriend and girlfriend. They were dancing as a family. Forever it would be so.

She pulled his face to her cheek, roughly, affectionately. A move she usually practised when drunk.

'Come here. Give us a kiss.'

'You've made me very happy, Mrs Joshi.'

'And you me, 'Mal. Even before this. I just never thought we'd get here.'

He wants to tell her now that they are still dancing as a family on this hard pub floor but cannot bear to see the disbelief that will appear on her face. How she will think that he is playing with her. More cruelty. If he was braver, able to pull her closer to him, he would push her fingers into his pockets and allow her to find it for herself: the retrieved hospital bracelet.

He never left us, you see. I was keeping him safe. There is a sense of something lost that we will always carry around, but this plastic in my pocket is the real thing. The almost sheer, tangible object that makes our baby concrete.

They could frame it if she wanted. Encase it in a clear resin block to sit on a bedroom shelf. He could run to gold-plating if she wanted; if that made it less painful. The parents of stillborn children get to take hand and footprints of their sleeping babies. Theirs should be similarly honoured.

Conflicting thoughts flood him. Will she allow the bracelet to be cut so that he too can wear him on a chain around his neck? Whether she can bring herself to share. Whether he can. He ponders the price of selfishness; whether the damage it will cause outweighs the continued comfort of having the complete coil safely in his pocket. He is a child pleased as punch with finders keepers. Needs more time with his treasure before disclosing.

Carrying a child will always be an unknown quantity to a man. No matter how closely the expectant mother communicates it, or the length of time he may attempt in a simulator suit, his depth of knowledge will only ever amount to a fraction of the real experience. He has felt her stomach, read every leaflet but still knows nothing.

A bracelet means nothing. Claud is dead on her feet, shuffles as if blindfold. The last song has mixed into the next, something dance-y and unsuitable, but he does not release her. She is the conduit for his solace; a flesh-and-blood lightning conductor. It is a poor substitute for the real thing but he is past caring. This is all he has. With one hand in his pocket he clutches at the plastic between his fingers and wishes for a heartbeat.

'When I was changing,' she says now, 'I had a look inside that box that Mum won at the tombola. It was a bell. Like the ones Morris dancers wear. What do you think she's going to do with it?'

'Give us a turn at dinner? Don't know. They're supposed to be lucky aren't they, those bells?'

'A couple of rattles over our heads to bring us good luck.'

'Would you turn your back on an offer of good luck?' he asks, seeing that she needs to be pulled out of herself;

chewing hard on the inside of her mouth in pained concentration.

'No. Not right now.'

⁂

He leads her outside to the Green. Holding her hand as lamp-light guides them to the spot. She is quietly submissive. The strength of her trust can be read through her grasp: firmer than he realized; tenacious to the end.

They should be shivering as the sharpness of the early evening air hits them but the last round of drinks has coated their insides with a vigorous, acidic fire. Even Claud, encouraged by her movements on the dance floor, made some headway into her red wine; two big gulps for courage, then slower and measured sipping once her taste for it returned.

The alcohol has brought looseness to her movements. Her steps are light and there is fluidity to her left arm as she gently swings his hand as they walk. It recalls the confidence of his glory days, back when he was a late teenager; when the casualness of walking hand in hand with a girl could give him all manner of strength. How the gesture itself, both shy and commanding, promised all manner of possibilities; all pleasurable ones that made him feel alive.

Past the pub lamp's radius, a third of the way into the

Green, they find their footsteps melting into blue-black. The terrain underfoot is firm if not entirely smooth. There are no sudden dips to mind, but there are smallish holes dotted around from the dogs which he stumbles into. When she pulls her weight back to balance him, he imagines being saved from sinking sands, or drowning. The way he has acted today, she could just have easily left him.

'Where are we going? If you're looking to get home it's the opposite way.'

'Almost there. You'll see.'

Tramping on damp grass. Grateful, she says, for wearing a pair of Liz's joggers instead of her patent heeled boots. Everything about her gear is practical and outdoorsy, almost as if she knew they would end up here, walking into black.

That afternoon, at the Herald, the Green felt a toy town in its scale: a landscaped miniature amid the wild growth of the working countryside surrounding it. In darkness, it becomes epic. He feels the openness of their surroundings rushing past his shoulders, somehow unclamping all that has knotted and twisted inside him. Black footsteps casting shadows he had not anticipated. Black on deep navy; black on black.

Stealing a glance behind he sees how a shadow has also fallen across the right side of her face; his too, he presumes. They are two half moons walking towards a possible salvation, about to embark upon a spontaneous, hopeful experiment.

It came to him during the last dance, after she stopped crying. It did not matter what she told him: her eating a prawn sandwich on Thursday lunchtime because she had been obsessing over it to the point of worship. The prawns had nothing to do with what happened. He was more cowed by the way she kept it to herself and let the secret fester until it grew to an illogical magnitude. Ashamed really, that he had not had the sense there was something to pull out of her.

'I'd been pining for the taste for days. Dreaming all week of that sweetness. When I saw the platter at the working lunch, something snapped. And I was conscious of people watching me, even though none of them knew I was pregnant, but I still ate it very quickly because of that. I had two triangles; one after another. And what made it really bad was that they didn't taste of anything!'

Clarity arrives in the worst way: through her inconsolable tears. What was needed, he sees, what had been missing all day, was support from a force that would not lay blame with shellfish or uncomprehending husbands. A higher power. There was no point in converting religion, no reason in forcing yourself into the realm of whether belief was actually possible, if those processes could not be called upon during these rootless moments.

The Church was never for him. A wedding present to

her family that's all. Even the poor conversion vicar saw that. Ma and Puppa had lost all faith in him praying to the blue and grey gods that childhood incredulity had long since marked incomprehensible. But something *was* out there, had to be, otherwise how else could they make sense of this? The loss could be explained by science; the healing, not.

'Why do you think people turn to religion in hard times? As a last resort or because they actually get something out of it?'

'If you wanted the Church you're the wrong way, too.'

'I'm not talking about the Church. I'm asking whether you believe.'

'In what?'

'Something outside of ourselves. Think about it.'

Their footsteps become shorter because she is tired and falls a further pace back, stretching their hold to its end point. He moderates himself accordingly, wanting to reach it as soon as possible but without dragging her like a caveman. She must be open and willing to try.

As they pause for her to catch her breath he feels something running over his foot. The tiny movement of a mouse. Its patter across the top of his brogue, less rhythmic, and more a scrabble to somewhere more urgent, strikes him with dumb gratitude. It is an experience that seems impossible had they been in Richmond, even with the scores of rats flooding the tangled miles of drainage.

They are alive in the world, and harnessed to a natural cycle. What they lack in understanding can be gained by learning to command what they have. They are alive, for fuck's sake. Anything is possible.

'We lit a bonfire here when we were sixteen. Night of the village hall Halloween party. Me and Rory and couple of others. Pissed out of our faces.'

'What is it with you and fires?'

'Don't know. If you burn the hell out of something you leave something good behind. Something sweeter. Those pujas your mum does. They always start with a flame.'

'The Catholic Church. They're big on candles.'

'And the Jewish Sabbath.'

'So you're saying that we should start a fire?'

She laughs, as sweet as the ashes she remembers; turning towards him so that the shadow finally falls from her eyes.

'It's something.'

They see the pole before they walk into it; its flat top illuminated by scatterings of village light, and a fistful of stars blearily peeping through the bank of cloud.

'This is where we dance round the maypole, is it, 'Mal?'

'No, but we could touch it and get some of its energy. Put your palms on it like this, see? Flat. Both hands.'

His feet are planted firm and wide apart as he does so. Something about the preparing athlete in his posture: head bowed for a few moments and then gradually raised, so that his eyes meet the pole's highest reaches. He remains unaware that this is what he set out to do until his eye catches the brass ring that clenches the top. Waiting for its reflection, a glint that indicates acknowledgement; approval.

Claud circles him for a few minutes, appraising his movement. He sees on her face, each time he lifts his head from its natural meditative position, an expression of surprise mellowing into a studied wonderment. Through all of their marriage, she never thought him capable.

Though he waits for a cascade of tutting to reach his ears he knows there will be none. She joins him, silently and without question; knowing the impact will be lost if she does not join forces and place herself opposite. The effort shows in the flare of her nostrils, suggesting a re-enactment of locked horns, before she allows her body to relax.

The pole brings them into sync. They have the wind and the trees and the racket from the pub as their white noise. Instead, they acquiesce to a soundtrack taken from bed: of gentle, muscular breathing, and of the clicks and rolls of the other's body.

'I wanted to call him Evan Neel. With the Indian spelling. Two Es,' she says after a time.

'So you thought he was a boy, too?'

'From the first moment I found out. I can't explain it. Isn't that strange?'

'Medicine can answer so many things, but the reason for some senses, those gut feelings, can never be traced.'

'What about you? What would you have named our son?'

'Haroon. It's Arabic. My parents would've hated it. More coals heaped onto the identity crisis.'

'I like yours better. Haroon. Beautiful name for a baby.'

It takes little for the scant light to fade: a thicker patch of cloud settling over the Green; curtains drawn in one of the several upstair windows of the cottages opposite the pub. The thick darkness renders them invisible to each other, bar hands on the pole and the outline of their forearms. He follows her lead. Still standing, heads staying bent. Hands now clasped round the pole, prayer-style.

'What do you feel, Claud?'

'That the pole's getting hotter.'

'It's our body heat. Means we've still got blood running through us.'

'What else?'

'I keep wondering how many others have done what we're doing. Stood here to ask for something. This afternoon I saw the village dogs sniffing around this pole, cocking their leg up probably, but that doesn't detract from what it is.'

'Is this what it takes? For us to have another baby?'

'Could be.'

'I'm not sure I believe it.'

'What else is there?'

He feels the trembling in her hands. A fear of the future; both the immediate and what lies further; what is wished for.

Heads bowed, they wait.

ACKNOWLEDGEMENTS

Thanks to: Stan; Karthika V.K., Shantanu Ray Chaudhuri, and all at HarperCollins India; Tabish Khair; Stuart Evers, Nikesh Shukla, Gavin James Bower, Lee Rourke; Alex Clark, Jake Arnott, Ian McMillan, Boyd Hilton, Will Ashon, Edmund White; my family.